THE ICE IS S

by the same author

SEPARATE TRACKS
HER LIVING IMAGE

THE ICE IS SINGING

Jane Rogers

faber and faber

LONDON · BOSTON

First published in 1987
by Faber and Faber Limited
3 Queen Square London WC1N 3AU
This paperback edition first published in 1988

Typeset by Goodfellow & Egan, Cambridge
Printed in Great Britain by
Richard Clay Ltd, Bungay, Suffolk
All rights reserved

© Jane Rogers, 1987

*This book is sold subject to the condition that it shall not, by way of trade
or otherwise, be lent, resold, hired out or otherwise circulated without the
publisher's prior consent in any form of binding or cover other than that
in which it is published and without a similar condition including
this condition being imposed on the subsequent purchaser.*

British Library Cataloguing in Publication Data

Rogers, Jane, *1952–*
The Ice is singing.
I. Title
923'.914[F]   PR6068.0346
ISBN 0-571-15230-9

Marion's journal and stories, February 2 – March 8 1986

Part of *The Ice is Singing* was written while I was Writer in Residence at Northern College, Barnsley, in 1985–6. I would like to thank Northern College and the Arts Council of Great Britain.

The characters in this book are fictional, and bear no relation to any person living or dead.

Jane Rogers

There were a lot of cars. It took me by surprise. Moving very fast. They swerve in and out. Or stop, or turn. As if they know exactly where they're going.

I was clear. The twins were asleep. I was perfectly clear. I started the engine, and backed on to the road in one manoeuvre, clean and mechanical. Moved the gearstick from first down to second, up and across to third, straight down to fourth. No sticking or crunching. Needle creeping across the clock. When I got to the end of the road I had to turn right, towards the motorway. But the bright headlights were moving too fast. I couldn't judge their speed. I stopped there watching. A car behind me hooted repeatedly. After a while I accelerated forwards into the road, and turned into a lane. More of them hooted at me, one screeched its brakes.

I tried to drive a straight line. Dazzling lights appeared quite suddenly out of the blackness both in front of and behind me, making me wobble. Those behind came up fast and just when I thought they would burst right through the back window they swerved out and roared past me. Their red tail-lights dived into the dark space of road I was driving towards.

I thought it would be best to stop. It was not possible to reach the side because they were passing on my left and right. I stopped in the middle, switching on the hazard-lights. The stream of cars divided easily around me and flowed on. Their moving lights made lines across the darkness. Ruth has a time-lapse photo of New York at night. The moving lights of vehicles have left trails across the picture. I thought, it would be easy to drive those streets, following the red and gold threads that hang suspended in the black air. To be strung in place like a bead.

1

Later on the traffic died down. When the road behind me seemed empty I started off again. It's like riding a bicycle, you have to keep going. I can't have driven at night for a long time. Gradually I built up speed.

It's warm in here. Someone's vacuuming the corridor. Outside it has snowed, quite heavily.

Monday February 3

I drove on up the motorway. There is snow lying, it makes the light strange. I'm driving through fluorescent tubes. The motorway was full of cars and slow. In places, like a conveyor belt. At a garage I filled the tank.

Driving is more like skating now. At times I can pull out and swoop past someone, skimming gracefully back into position in front of them. The car seems more responsive, it likes to swoop and glide quickly. It is engaging my concentration, I do not think about anything else. I feel well; I feel quite clear. I do everything right. Eat, go to bed, eat. When I slept I dreamed I was still driving.

My head is full of emptiness, a white eggshell. I drive in silence to keep it so. The radio is trouble. Snow light is filling up my eyes, they are scoured white. I drive blind, but the road is a clear black line and not hard to follow. Keeping moving seems the best thing to do. I move to keep blank (it works); driving all day with a ball of thoughts and feelings rolling along behind me, ready to crush, a carelessly chucked giant's marble.

Tonight I am staying in a small cluttered room, with a china dog, amongst other things, on the mantelpiece. There is no phone.

Today I drove around smaller roads. They are clear, wet black ribbons twisting over a white landscape. On these country roads I notice that the snow does not cover the land so much as reveal it. As if it was stripped naked. You see its curves; the way a field rim turns up in a pout to a hedge; the slow undulation between two hilltops; the sliding curve of flank in a huge white expanse of field. The snow strips it of distractions and colour, flattens weeds and tall grass, and absorbs back into the shape of the surface the harsh outlines of rocks, ruined ploughs, piles of fencing and rotting bales. All detail is concealed, to reveal the sensuous shape of the whole. Trees and stone walls are all that show up, the trees bare, black and scratchy-spindly, shocking tufts of coarse black pubic hair in the folds and valleys of the body. Stone walls make black lines fractured by white, outlining shapes, emphasizing the creases between limbs. The body that lies around me is huge. I crawl across it like an ant on a Henry Moore figure, lost between voluptuous swellings.

A story.

A Natural Father

The school playground was fenced with green plastic-coated wire mesh, in diamond shapes, eight foot or so high. To prevent intruders, perhaps – or stop the children, like creatures in a zoo, from escaping. He stood right next to the wire, close enough so that each eye was looking through a separate diamond-shaped space. As he leant forward to stare, silently imploring the clusters of children by the wall, and round the boilerhouse, to break up and reveal themselves, his hands came up and gripped the wire either side of his staring face. She wasn't there at first. His clenched hands were sweating. He stood rigid, willing her to appear.

Then from around a corner – or skipping out from the middle of a crowd right under his nose – would come the yellow-white fluff of hair, framing the terrible sweet face. There she was.

She never looked at him. She seemed to be happy, engaged with other children. Laughing, or being chased, or intent in intimate conversation. Once he had spotted her it was impossible to lose sight of her; she was the only child in the playground with hair so blonde it was nearly white – silver in some lights, a warm pale-yellow silver, like early morning sunshine, not the sad grey-silver of old age. Silver Top, Duck's Fluff, Dandelion Clock, were names he had called her. Now she was bigger, with knobbly schoolgirl knees beneath her pleated skirt.

He hung immobile against the fence, hot and weak, till the bell was rung at one. The children ran to the doorway and he watched her light till the crowd of taller children pressing round her blotted it out.

Miss Haughton had been headmistress of Castle Hill Primary for eighteen years. She had seen most things, in her time. And she had seen men who hung in the shadows at the far end of the playground, following her children with eating eyes. This one was different because he came right up to the fence. In fact from the window of her office it looked as if he were lying, spreadeagled, against the fence. Like a man in a prison camp, she thought.

They should all be in prison. They should all be in prison, the filthy creatures, with their beastly appetites. Besides, he was damaging her fence. His whole weight was pressing against it. Soon it would begin to sag between its supports and have to be renewed. The children knew they mustn't lean or climb on it. You'd think a grown man would have more sense.

The next time she spotted him she put down her roll of sugar paper, took the drawing pins from between her teeth, and marched straight out to send him packing.

'If I see you loitering here again I shall call the police. Do you understand? These children are under my protection.'

The man turned pale when she spoke to him. The children had fallen in behind her and semi-circled her, iron filings round a magnet, as she faced him. A little girl with white-blonde hair stood there open-mouthed, staring at the strange man. He turned and fled.

His wife had been animated, like the child. It was one of the things that had attracted him to her. She was always engaged, laughing and chattering to other people. She seemed to have boundless energy. When they married he found it less attractive, because she was such a fly-by-night. She would start one project with all the enthusiasm in the world, and then lose interest. The house was full of half-finished things: half-made curtains, half-knitted jumpers, half-written letters. Being slow and thorough himself, he was finally irritated by her wilful skittishness. And, of course, vice versa. By the time he had painstakingly finished off the fitted cupboards in the kitchen, two months after she'd helped him choose the design, she could no longer stand the sight of the wretched things.

A couple of years passed. They both wanted children. They had planned to start a family as soon as they married, but nothing happened. Sometimes when things were going badly between them he thought it was just as well. At other times he thought a baby might help. She went to the doctor's and a slow round of tests was started up. Odd hospital appointments here and there, and people telling them there was plenty of time yet. She seemed to make it more her concern than his; and when it would not be solved in a day or a single visit to the hospital, she lost patience. They rarely talked about it, though they made love often – it was the only activity in which they didn't exasperate each other.

He began to long for a child. Not knowingly, but with a dull subconscious pang of loss. He wanted something he could watch and cherish and receive warmth from, like the slow steady glow of a fire; instead of the intricate, inanimate objects his life was devoted to at work, and at home in the car, the decorating, the fitting of wardrobes. He wanted someone who would grow in his warmth, to whom he could give the slow burning love which was locked away from his wife's impatience. Loneliness was like an absence following him. There was no security between himself and Elizabeth.

Their lives were locked in a pattern of separateness. During the week they each worked; in the evenings he watched telly and she went to her evening classes. At weekends he tinkered with the car and worked on the house, while she shopped, visited friends, came and went untidily, leaving doors open, and half-finished cups of coffee, and dishes in the sink. Knowing that she was as unhappy as he was the only thing that made him able to bear her behaviour.

When she told him she was pregnant he was past believing it. It was too good to be true. They had been trying for three and a half years.

He was so happy he didn't know how to express it, and hardly dared to for fear of it vanishing. He started work on the baby's room, stripping, sanding, painting; slow and thorough. She was quieter and often seemed tired; being able to wait on her and bring her things eased his desire to love her. He thought she was never so beautiful as when she pregnant.

He went to the hospital with her when she started in labour, but towards the end they sent him out, because they needed to use forceps. The midwife said Elizabeth wasn't pushing hard enough. He stood in the room where they put him in a blaze of fear, praying to the God he hadn't believed in since junior school. If you let them be all right, I don't care what happens. You can do anything you like to me afterwards, I won't mind. Just let them both be all right, please God.

The baby (Amanda) was born with clean white hair, and a screwed-up kitten's face. David cried when he saw her. And when he dared to cuddle her close enough to feel the living heat of her small, determined body, the cold space of loss that he had carried inside himself for years blazed up with an answering warmth.

Elizabeth was an erratic mother. She fed the child and looked after her well enough, but sometimes she wanted to do nothing but pet and fondle her – at others the baby must be banished to her cot for hours on end, to learn to sleep and get into a routine. Crisis followed crisis: over feeding (breast, followed after two weeks by bottle), colic, non-sleeping, nappy rash, dummies versus thumbs, and so on. Gradually David gained confidence, and began to infiltrate Elizabeth's sloppinesses with his own methodical preparations. He cleaned the bottles, sterilized them and mixed up new feeds. With a patience he recognized as scheming – perhaps evil – he waited for Elizabeth to get tired of her new toy. Soon he had taken over the night-time feeds. He was at work all day, and became so tired he often hallucinated, but at night he was awake, ready with Amanda's feeds, ready to change and cuddle and play with her. Alongside the growing intensity of his adoration for Amanda mushroomed a terrible fear for her. He began to imagine all sorts of things going wrong while he was out – Elizabeth leaving her dangerously near the edge of the bed, or Amanda choking in her sleep and Elizabeth not noticing. He was haunted by tales of cot deaths and infantile diseases.

Elizabeth, maddened by his fussing over the child, flared up and attacked him.

'Look at yourself. You never sleep. You never even look up. You scuttle about from work to the baby to work again, with great bags under your eyes, like some sort of maniac. It's impossible to hold a conversation with you. You're insane.'

She insisted that he leave the baby to her for a few nights, and he did so, taking sleeping pills to prevent himself lying listening for the cries that Elizabeth might not hear. Amanda survived. She was smiling now, and waving her arms above the blankets when she woke.

There began to be a balance between David and Elizabeth, as he recognized that she wouldn't actually let the child starve, and she accepted that it was useful if he fed the child in the evenings and at night. It meant she could go out.

When Amanda was nearly one, Elizabeth made an announcement which was as startling as the news of her pregnancy had been. David had put Amanda to bed and was having his tea. Elizabeth, who was going out, had already had hers.

'I want a divorce. I've met someone else and he wants to marry me.'

She treated David's astonished questioning with contempt.

'Well, if you didn't know you must be blind. It won't make a damn of difference to you – Amanda's the only thing in the world you care about anyway.'

'Yes, I've known him a while. I've known him two years, if you must know – on and off.'

When she'd gone out David sat staring at the dirty table. He was glad she went out. He wanted to hit her. He wanted to hit her face and punch her belly and hurt her. That was the only thing he could think of. Hitting both of them with all his strength. The want seemed to swell and he raised his fist and brought it down with all his force on the table. Two plates fell off and shattered, and the milk fell over, spilling everywhere. His fist hurt.

He was not a man to analyse feelings. When the desire to hit her stopped being a physical need, he methodically tidied and swept the kitchen. Then he went and looked at Amanda sleeping. It was Amanda he cared about. He wouldn't care about Elizabeth, he wouldn't even interest himself in what the bitch did. She was finished, as far as he was concerned. It was Amanda he loved.

When Elizabeth returned later that night he was perfectly controlled. Speaking politely and distantly he began to discuss the settlement of their joint finances. He proposed that she move out immediately. Amanda would continue to live with him but he would deliver her to Elizabeth in the mornings when he went to work, and collect her on his way home. He would stay in the house and buy her half of the joint mortgage from her. Elizabeth, who had visibly been crying, flew into an uncontrolled rage, calling him a bastard and throwing her shoes at him.

'I wish I'd never married you. I wish I'd never seen you!' she screamed. 'You don't know what love is. You've never loved me, you've never cared about me. Only the cupboards and the car and the fucking wallpaper. You won't love Mandy either, when she starts to be a person – she'll see through you. You're incapable of love!'

He didn't see what she had to be so upset about, since she was getting her own way and leaving. He went to bed and when she followed him with her weeping and accusations he shifted to the spare room.

Elizabeth moved out. The quality of David's life improved almost immediately. He was an organized man, and with no one else interfering in the house, he could make it run like a machine. He shopped during his lunch-hour, and devoted the evenings to Amanda. She was walking now, and learning to talk. Her company was a constant source of delight. When he called for her she would go into a frenzy of excitement, clapping her hands and shouting, 'Da da da da!' She giggled uproariously at him when he pulled faces; they had a game where he would chase her round the sofa on all fours, roaring, and soon he had only to pretend to crouch down, to send her into a paroxysm of laughter.

At weekends he took her out, planning outings to zoos and parks to delight her. When old ladies commented on how pretty and clever she was he glowed with pleasure. People were always remarking on her beautiful hair, which grew longer and more fly-away, without ever changing its silver-blonde colour. He called her Silver Top, Duck's Fluff, Dandelion Clock.

As if he had been turned on a giant wheel, he entered again into a terrible state of anxiety about Elizabeth's care of Amanda. Elizabeth might let her run out on to the road. She might fall downstairs. He could see her hurt, maimed, unconscious on a hospital bed; she was only safe when she was with him. And when the child fell asleep, exhausted, at 8.30 or 9 p.m., he resented all the waking daytime hours of her Elizabeth had enjoyed.

He considered leaving his job. If he gave up work . . . It would only be for three years anyway. Amanda could start school at four and a half. It wasn't long – and he could sell the car, and do odd pieces of carpentry at home, at nights. He had savings. Maybe he could persuade Elizabeth to wait for her money from the mortgage, till Amanda was five. The new man was well off, to judge by the size of his house.

He realized that Amanda greeted Elizabeth with enthusiasm when he took her back in the mornings. She did like her mother. Would it harm her to lose contact? From the opulence of his imagined full days and nights with her, he considered letting her go to Elizabeth for the odd weekend.

He gave six weeks' notice at work before he'd even spoken to Elizabeth. He didn't want the confrontation. But he was also quite sure that he would get what he wanted. If Elizabeth refused, he would go to court and get proper custody. He was the injured party in the whole affair – and had clearly established more rights to Mandy through his continued care of her. There was no way he could lose.

He finally told Elizabeth one morning as he dropped Amanda off, that he'd like to talk to her that evening. At 6 p.m. she ushered him into an untidy, expensively furnished lounge. As she turned to open the door in front of him he realized, with a jolt, that she was pregnant again.

So much the better. She'd have no need to fight for Amanda now – she'd have a new baby all to herself. It hadn't taken them long, had it. It hadn't taken them three bloody years.

She sat down and asked him, quite formally, to sit. He tried not to look at her. He was just starting to speak when the door opened and a man's blond head peered round and said, 'Sorry!' before withdrawing.

David started again. 'I've come to see you about Amanda.'

She nodded distantly. He imagined the shape of her belly under her smock, and his hands remembered the feel of her skin, stretched tight and silky-smooth. It was impossible that he should be speaking to her like this – in another man's house. He had to close his eyes to steady himself and tell himself with all his concentration, 'She is a bitch and I don't care about her. She is nothing to me.' His hands, clenched on the arms of the chair, were sweating horribly. He wondered where Amanda was. It would be easier if he could see her.

'I'm stopping work. Given in my notice. I want to – you to – I want you to let me have Amanda. I'll look after her in the days too. You can see her – but I want her. It's only fair. You can see that.' Blurted out, not like any of the speeches he had planned. He was burning up. What was it? He didn't even know what it was that was sending waves of hot panic beating through his flesh.

Elizabeth seemed composed. She spoke in a low voice. 'Look, I've got something to tell you, David, and I should have told you before. I've been putting it off because I didn't want to upset you. But there's nothing else I can do, I'm afraid. I didn't –' She faltered, and he suddenly realized that far from being composed she too was terrified, on the edge of tears. Her voice dropped even lower and he had to crouch forward to hear her. 'When I moved in with Mark he guessed something which I'd never thought of. He hadn't really seen her before, you see. But when he saw Amanda – properly – he guessed.' She came to a complete stop. David was paralysed. The 'WHAT?' of rage inside him could not come out, and lodged in his throat like a brick. At last she went on.

'It's the hair, you see. It's so unusual. It would have been such a coincidence. And yours and mine both brown . . .'

Noise. Of roaring. Inside a furnace roaring up with a huge burning lion maw to swallow into red heat.

As it subsided she'd been talking on ' . . . because I didn't, honestly, it never entered my head; he said, well, you can prove it. So he took her to the doctor's and had a blood test.'

Roaring again, blocking her out. Red coming up before the eyes darkening to black. The white speaking senseless face blotted out, then hanging like a puppet gibbering before him. The mouth went on opening and closing, the face contorting, as he watched. She was crying. She was talking. 'I'm sorry. I'm sorry, David. I didn't know, I promise you. You can – if you want you can see her – Mark won't mind – if you want to see her sometimes.'

Without knowing how or where the strength came from he got out of the house, Elizabeth following him and crying at him all the time. At the door she caught his arm and he pushed her back, and stumbled down the steps. She shrank back into the hallway, staring at him. As he turned on to the pavement the corner of his eye was seared by a flash of white hair at the bedroom window.

He had never seen Amanda again. Except secretly, through fences. And the schoolteacher was right. Carry on like that and he'd turn into one of those perverts, be no better than them. Frightening a little girl at the school gate, with the ugly exposure of his crippling love.

I am telling stories. In a chipboard cupboard of a room six floors up a cement column, with hot dry air and nylon sheets. The room is so full of electricity that I have adapted to walking slowly, avoiding contacts. My hair crackles, the dry skin on my face is peeling. My lip bleeds.

I am here, not there. There are the twins, Paul and Penny, giggling crying slavering slopping their food sucking their thumbs. Paul sobs in his sleep, Penny moans. My babies who have sucked my breasts and grown in my flesh, pieces of me, my belly my heart.

I am sitting six floors up with a window over the motorway to hills; a five-star view in a one-star room. Snow. Total snow, not London snow. Snow on road ditch hill tree roof cloud car field. I am not –

Not a diary not a journal. Not Marion, not a sniff or spit or print of her. In my cement tower (once doubtless white as an ivory but now yellowing grey as decayed teeth, a tower for my times, the days of ivory – like the golden age – being gone) I sit. Sit, wait, woman in a tower. Like Mariana in her moated grange. No, Rapunzel, gone bald. Stuck up a tower for good.

No games. Here. Nylon sheets, lemon. Two blankets, off white. Nylon quilted bedspread, pink floral. Grey fleck carpet. Woodchip off-white walls. Fitted white-wood wardrobe and shelves, white washbasin, and mirror. Bedside coffee table (supporting lamp) of such generous proportions that this exercise of arm and pen is possible. I sit on the floor under the window, back against the bed, legs outstretched beneath the table. Writing on a new block of A4 ruled feint (wide).

Me. No Penny no Paul No Ruth No Vi no Gareth. Me.

Yes, inescapably me. Not Marion, she says. Not a stiff or— But her sniffs and spits are all over David and Amanda. She has pummelled him into shape – hasn't she? With her hammy fists, he's moulded and sticky as dough, paddled with the prints of her flat-edged fingers. Listen.

'He began to long for a child. Not knowingly, but with a dull subconscious pang of loss.' He didn't know (she says). But Marion knows. Mother knows what's wrong before you know yourself. She names the pain. She identifies it, telling herself that thus it can be remedied, later in the story. Suggesting to herself – comforting herself – deluding herself again – that things follow on, make sense, have remedies.

Perhaps she wanted a good wallow. Nothing like someone else's troubles. Liberally doused with ketchup, with 'slow burning love'. Great towering passions, in red and black cloaks. She doesn't feel secure unless she thinks they're there.

Instead of real things. Little things, that lurk and move quick and don't make sense. They resist explanation. They won't stand still to have metaphors hung round their necks like mayoral chains. Quick, dart, lurk. They've gone.

Marion. Whatever she writes. She might as well stop now.

Fri. 7

Snow. More snow every day. Many roads are blocked. I thread my way along those that have been cleared; even in frost they remain wet because of the salt. The verges, heaped high with snow-plough packed snow, are ruined and blackened like a building after fire. On the other side of hedge or wall the white begins, snow clear to the next blobbed wall. There are no colours in this landscape, it is black and white, and even the black is faded – grey black, faint black: whiteness of snow overpowers all, bleaching the eye, leeching colour.

My eyes are suffering; they ache, and at times white masses seem to shift before them, even when I'm not driving. The world seems slippery to them, they can't get a grip on it. Perhaps I should buy some sunglasses. My neck and shoulders ache as well. I need to take a rest from driving.

You talk rubbish. A tube of chemicals fizzing, changing colour by the minute. Lions pace. Pigs chew. Marion drives. It's Nature's way, my dear – survival. Do you think you've made a choice? Bid for freedom, escape? Can you escape your own nature, your own substance, the sloppy porridge of cells which are your construction, flesh and bones? All they're programmed for is to keep you alive – they don't care how.

1. Lion. In a cage, paces. Hormones thereby released dull its anxiety, keep it sane.

2. Pig. (More satisfyingly, more symbolically) in a factory farm, secured in its stall with chains, chews them. Day and night, obsessively. Survives, pain of captivity blunted, high on the heroin substitute its body manufactures in response to chain-chewing. Remove its chains, it cracks up: beats it brains out against the walls.

3. Marion. The case is less extreme. Drives. Brain pleasantly numbed from consideration of more serious matters.

Chemicals. Programmed to survive. All you are.

That's enough.

Sat. 8

At times I can go down in an eddy – down, down, below the static-noise surface, into the quiet spaces (underwater?) where vision is peculiarly clear. One thought one image leading to the next like slippery underwater rope I'm on a trail, can't let go in the dark clear depths for fear of total loss, but if it's possible to pursue the thought to its end (cave diver in the liquid hollows of the earth) then I will win –

What? No more than a journey of that length. Always at the end, finally, a rock wall, a crevice too narrow for my shoulders.

Strange changes in my body as I travel through no-time. I seem to swell and bloat like a drowned woman. My hands and feet have puffed up so that the skin is tight. Reasonably, I argue that it's due to hours of driving, sitting still, blood not circulating. My body remembers it as a sign of pregnancy. My aching eyes never recover from assaults of snow glare. And now my lips are dried and cracking like sun-baked mud. They too seem to have swollen; they are bursting through the old skin, which shrivels back, to be peeled absentmindedly by me as I drive. Today I peeled a section raw.

Reasonably, reasonably. The air outside is sharp and cold. Inside my car is hot and dry, the heater like a breath from the desert. My lips are simply dry. A sensible application of Vaseline or Lypsyl three times a day would sort them out. In the mirror I see a woman I've never met, with tiny squinting eyes and swollen bleeding lips.

My lips must be constantly touched. I find myself stroking the silken new skin; pressing them together and moistening the dry corners; brushing the back of my hand against them, peeling with my teeth the onion layers of old skin. I have picked foolishly at the scabs until they've bled again.

I am continuously aware of my lips. I feel them move and crack. I lick them to taste the blood. I can't rest, I can't leave them alone to heal. Last night I lay on my back with my hands clenched beneath me, to stop them stealing up to touch and peel my gigantic lips. I imagined I might unpick myself. Picking and picking, peeling back the skin, touching and brushing the moist new flesh, laying the backs of my fingernails against it, fretting at the edges of what is (already, for God's sake) a hole; I might unpick enough to find an end to pull – that would make the whole lot unravel.

They're a neat edge around a hole, lips. Like a button hole. We girls learnt button-hole stitch at junior school. Blanket stitch, the stitch for binding raw edges. Over and over goes the thread, passing the needle through each previous stitch's loop, linking them together to make an edge.

I circle it. Over and over (sewing or unpicking?) I painstakingly circle the hole. The world resolves itself into images and theories of lips.

Consider Lips

Mouth edges. The rims of darker skin that frame the hole into which go air drink food thumbs lollipops cigarettes nipples and other parts of other people's anatomies. Out from which come breath (used air) spit (lubricant and dissolver of those anatomies and lollipops) vomit (regurgitated food and drink) and words. Which have no counterpart in any of those things that go in. Except that words name them: identify them, ask for them, and so appear to own and control them all.

It's not all to do with going in and coming out, though – don't think of lips as just an entrance way. That would be to disregard their intrinsic beauty and agility. They are the face's leading actor. Curving in smiles and grins, stretching in exasperation, pursing in annoyance, hollowing to a thin round O of desolate misery, downturning at the corners in set lines of anticipated and fulfilled mediocrity and boredom. And when you touch them with

your fingers doesn't your skin wonder at their smooth-
ness and durability, their appearance and texture of
inside-the-body skin, which yet survives in the dry
outside? Their sex colour, the bruised pink-brown of all
hole-edges. Their luscious, curving shape, which makes
you want to lick them.

As for their movements, in speech alone their flexibility
is extraordinary. When Billie Whitelaw played Beckett on
TV, they filmed nothing but her speaking lips. Her lips
filled the screen with a life, a tension, a manipulation and
concatenation of muscle movements which was riveting;
awe-inspiring. The words formed by these lips were lost –
meaningless, insignificant – beside the movements which
formed them. Medium made mincemeat of message.

On another surface – the surface, say, of your body –
lips can mould, brush, skim, suck, infill any space or
crevice. Against your lips they can breathe, tremble, press,
grind, hold in open-mouthed suspension. Kiss.

Lips move; lips touch; lips signal. Lips are on the
outside for show, and on the most secret inside of your
mouth. Lips frame words that lie. Lips frame a hole that
wants to be filled.

My children's lips. My husband's lips. Lips that have
touched me.

Babies' lips.

They come ready pursed, as big from top to bottom as
they are from side to side. In age our mouths elongate –
wider and wider in grin or grim, both of which are similar
in that they are lines that know; alas, that know. A baby's
mouth knows and seeks to know nothing beyond nipple.
Ejected from warm wet inside to cold dry outside, from
darkness to light, from flesh-fluid suppleness to the
disparate harsh angles of metal, plastic and starched white
sheet, the baby wants home. Warmth. Wetness. Flesh.
Insides. Its body is nothing but an aimless sack, with
every nerve leading to its lips. Only its lips know how to

make it survive. Its lips slot and clamp like a vice over nipple. Nipple, source of warm wet nourishment, connection with mother's insides, meeting of flesh.

At the first closing of new-born Ruth's jaw on my breast I shouted in pain. If she could have sucked my nipple off and wormed her way back inside through the bloody hole it left, she'd have done it. A new-born baby's suck is a desperate thing. The mother's breast is the life-line, the life-hole. The greedy twins sucked me raw, till my nipples swelled and cracked. Little animals chewing at dugs; would tear the flesh and eat it if they could, if it would help them.

On the breast, a baby's lips (contrary to popular belief) do not form the shape that we call suck. Sucking goes on inside, further down the baby's maw. The lips are there for manipulation and control, making, in the course of feeding, a score of tiny adjustments of motion and position. The top lip closes over the flesh in a straight line, so that neither the pinky-brown of lip nor of areola is seen. The infant's top lip is a flat surface; when they grow older children's lips become fuller, but roundedness here would prevent that neat seam, one plane of flesh cleanly fitting another. The underlip is turned out, in a pout, around the underside of the nipple. When the first gush of milk stops and the baby requires more, it allows the nipple to slide very slightly out of its mouth. No longer sucking, it holds the nipple between jaws and applies with the lower lip an infinitesimal trembling motion. The upper lip remains still, a pressure point. The effect upon the nipple of being ever-so-slightly trembled from below is a tickling, turning to a tingling, turning in the mother's body to a sense of yearning which is satisfied by the sudden release of a hidden reserve of milk shooting through the breast. The lower lip stops trembling, slides quickly over the edge of the areola, to clamp in position and allow the open gullet to fill again with gushing milk.

Consider a child in distress. Not a baby, a child, with teeth and an appetite for crisps and gum. How is its unhappiness signalled? Eyes, yes, brimming with tears. But about the mouth? A trembling, a much-described, a clichéd wobbling of the lower lip. Baby wants more milk. Wants connection of blood-warm liquid flowing from her mother's body into her own. Wants comfort.

Can the trembling of a child's lip really be cured by the application of Germolene to a grazed knee, or a mouthful of Smarties? Most adult lips have given up, forgotten how to tremble. Never again will they close on flesh as close, as real, as one-with-them, as mother's breast. All others are substitutes. They seem to be – for a while, almost certainly are – as good, as potent to comfort and banish the dark. But they are not the real thing.

And the mother? She who has been the source of all love all comfort all warmth and wetness of milky breasts, through whose nipple holes have spun the white life-lines of liquid connecting still her child's belly with her own? What of her? I am a mother and a child, but write of comfort lost as a child.

Because the baby's love is for itself. It sucks and cries and demands and lays claim, in order to survive. Its huge self-love admits the existence of no other. Mother is home, food, warmth, life. Its love for its mother is its love of life itself, sweet life to be sucked from the source. The mother, who was herself a sucking baby once, knows her function. She is God, the source of life and happiness: and she is an old dried fruit to be spat away.

Sun. Feb. 9

My lips are so bad I haven't been out. I've passed the time writing nonsense, looking through the window, and pacing up and down. I want to get in the car again. I'm wearing gloves to stop myself from mauling my lips.

And the lips of my children, which feasted on my flesh, now curl or close tight at the sight of me. Only the twins grin and slaver; and as is only natural, they'll grow out of it.

No lips seek me. Like the housewife that I am, I start to unravel the old useless garment (starting from the site of the hole) in order to make new use of the rewound yarn. My lips spill words, phrases drip from the end of my pen, sentences flow out in a river.

Mon. Feb. 10

The car windows were encrusted with frost this morning – both inside and out. I tried rubbing it with a cloth, which was useless, then walked to a garage and bought some spray. The spray leaves a filmy coating on the glass, which the windscreen wipers smear without removing. I have had trouble focusing, because of this, all day.

I drove for an hour or two, in no particular direction, attracted by roads that promised wide views and few towns. But after a while I found myself coming back into industrial suburbs, the outskirts of Sheffield. I stopped and consulted the road map, because I felt quite clear about what I wanted today: space, snow, straight roads. Emptiness. I decided to head west, where the map showed an empty-looking area, sparsely crossed by roads – the Pennines. In an hour my road led me down into a tight dark town wedged between hills. The blackened stone of its buildings dripped and pressed in around me. There was a fine spray of sleet beating through the air, that melted when it hit street or windscreen. They'd forgotten to switch off a sign warning that the Manchester road was closed due to snow.

As I turned right at the foot of the steep hill out of Holmfirth, I imagined soaring up above the blackened stone walls and slate roofs, and looking down over the valley; if the mist and rain would let me. The wet black road was lined to the right by large Victorian houses, ponderous behind white gardens. The sleet became heavier, thickening up from transparency to whiteness, clotting into snow. And as I cleared the row of houses, breaking into countryside, the wind hit me from the north. The car shifted a foot or so across the surface of the road, where sleety snow was sticking lightly. The wipers were already on; I switched on the lights and the beams picked up two rods of moving air in front of me, as if the snowflakes were dancing atoms in a pyramid of solid matter. In the inch or two of clear screen following the wiper blade I saw the road (no longer even grey now, but white) curving up on ahead of me. I wasn't at the top. I considered the fact that it would probably be worse up there. Already the solid houses of Holmfirth seemed a long way back. I pressed down on the accelerator, and as I surged on round the next bend, noticed an uneasiness beneath the wheels. Gradually I realized that the deepening snow on the road was in layers, rutted with the passing of earlier traffic.

Above the engine noise the sound of the wind was a constant note – a screech across the metal surfaces of the car, a great howl across the invisibility of the moors, which I guessed must now stretch out all around me. Though I could see nothing. The fact that I could see nothing grew on me slowly. Slowly I realized that the eerie darkness in the car was due not just to the weather, but to the right-hand windows being completely plastered with snow. Odd powdery fragments of flakes danced in through the ventilation system. The atmosphere out there was solid with them. It was impossible to follow any difference caused by the movements of the wipers. They cleared the glass but did so to reveal air half an inch ahead, already clogged with streaming white dust. I slowed down. When I did so the feeling of slipping between ruts in the snow became more strong. I was not sure if I was on one side or in the middle of the road, straddling the tyre tracks of vehicles travelling in opposing directions.

I couldn't see the wall that had run alongside the road to my left. Perhaps now I was on the moors it had stopped. Perhaps it was still there but I just couldn't see it. Perhaps in its place there was a five hundred foot drop to a rocky streambed below. I had no idea. Nor, except when the wheels guided themselves by slipping down the packed sides of my predecessors' tracks and turning obediently to follow in the full depth of the ruts, did I know when the road was doing anything other than running straight ahead. There could be curves, hairpin bends. I could not see the road in front of my car.

I tried to remember whether anyone had passed me. There had been someone in front. He must be up there somewhere in the blind whiteness, extending the road before me. Or stopped dead in his tracks, thirty yards ahead.

I changed down to second gear, let my speed drop to below 10 m.p.h. I was beginning to lose any sense of the road at all. I was slipping and skidding frequently. I noticed I was hot – in fact, sweating. My hands on the wheel were sticky. I switched off the car heater. Part of me was braced, at each bump and slither, to go on falling – off, over, away. To nothing.

I didn't decide to stop. But I did stop. My foot lifted itself off the accelerator, my left hand moved the gearstick across to neutral and reached down to yank up the handbrake. The car stopped. The bumping and slithering underwheel stopped, although the solid white wind continued to streak across my windscreen. I turned off the engine. The howl of the wind rendered its absence unnoticeable. The window wipers stopped, and the inside of the car darkened a shade. The atmosphere had congealed. Not like darkness, which is penetrable by light. Not like water which, though solid, is clear. This was solid and opaque; like being buried, like soil. Buried alive in whiteness. The wind was pummelling the car from the right, and it shivered and trembled in the force of the gusts, as a larger vehicle will shudder at the idling of its own engine.

I sat still, hands on the wheel. I was still hot. The windscreen was solid now, dark. I tried to imagine what my car would look like from outside. How long it would take it to lose its shape. Then I did something stupid – pushed down the handle and tried to open the door. My weight forced it open an inch or two, before the power of the wind slammed it again. The car was filled with a flurry of snow, which flew all over my face and clothes, and melted on me. The air was ice cold. I don't know what I had intended. Even if I had been able to open the door – clearly – it would be madness to get out. There was nothing there. Nothing but blizzard.

I was cold now. I couldn't have come more than five miles from Holmfirth. Five miles from wet black roads, houses, shops, mothers hurrying their children home from school. Five miles from pubs and boutiques, four miles up the road from solid burghers' houses with gas central heating and wall-to-wall berber. On other roads there are traffic jams; people wait, their windows misting up impatiently, the soft beating of their windscreen wipers ticking off the time to tea. I was as far away as Antarctica. I was cold. I turned on the engine.

I needn't have come this way. I could have seen – I did see. Sickeningly, I remember the 'Road closed' sign. I saw it. Discounted it and drove on. I look at my watch. Four ten. Soon it will be dark. It will be pitch dark in the car,

25

then; not just dark, but black. I have no torch. Nor blanket. Nor drink. I have half a packet of Polos. I remember that people can die through sitting in cars with the engines on. Something to do with the fumes.

While I sit there, very still, in my bubble of space under my snowdrift, and balk and panic, and still find my predicament incredible – I am watching.

Watching Marion, who has stupidly (unthinkingly – perhaps uncaringly) endangered her life. Whose cold flesh is sweating; whose ears are tensed and intent on the whine of the wind (muffled now), searching its note for any hint (impossible to hear) of other noise that might mean rescue; whose aching snow-blind eyes are riveted on the dark solid mass beyond her windscreen, willing it to shift; a compartment of whose racing, panic-stricken mind is calmly planning Girl Guide methods of survival, considering how long it will take to use up the air in the car, and how a breathing tube might be inserted through the snow; searching her memory for weather forecasts she might have casually overheard at breakfast. Watching Marion who is very intent on not dying. Who wanders the countryside professing to seek blankness – running scared from a burial in clean white snow. And indeed, in part of her head, grovelling (to a swiftly resurrected God) for her rebellion. For her present death can be seen only as just reward for her ingratitude. If she had valued her life, she would not have endangered it.

The irony is, of course, that I did not wilfully endanger it today. I am here, now, buried alive, not by choice but by accident.

I was there for two hours. The wind must have dropped because I heard the noise of the plough before I saw anything – or felt, rather than heard, the deep vibration of its engine. He was passing to my right, very slowly. I turned on my engine and pressed the horn, which made a tinny, muffled sound. I pressed the handle and flung my weight against the door, which was packed solid with snow. It swung open and I half-fell out with force of my push. The snow was falling in flakes – vertically, from sky to ground. A different substance altogether. In the dim blue light I could see that the plough had cleared half the road, passing me with inches to spare. He was already lost in the darkness ahead, had not even noticed my buried shape. I flailed at the snow above the bonnet with both arms, and dug out a patch of windscreen. I put the car into first gear, turned the wheels to the right, and pressed the accelerator. It moved, almost easily, out of its snowdrift and on to the cleared road. The wheels did not stick or skid or spin. They turned, and took me on to solid tarmac. I got out and cleared the windows again, put on my lights and slowly, carefully, gratefully, followed the snow-plough on over the moors and down the winding descent to a village called Greenfield.

Tues. 11

Today she's sorry for herself. No driving. Hollowed out, sunken, collapsing inwards. Sees herself: Marion, a silly woman stuck in a metal case under a layer of snow on top of a hill, afraid of dying. A mindless scuttler along roads.

Keeping moving. Does she think she's driving towards freedom, escape? That because she's driving she's going somewhere? What will there be at the end of the long narrow road? Does she expect to arrive at flowery fields of freedom? Uninterrupted peace, stillness, after the harass-ment of continual motion? Sounds like she's going to heaven.

But when that kind white stillness came down around you, Marion, padding and wedging you in peace – oh sister, when the snowy angels stretched out their spotless arms to clasp you to the breast of heaven –

she didn't want. Not at all. No intention of reaching journey's end, thank you. No interest in peace and freedom. No desire for tranquillity or angel choirs.

Trapped in motion like a rat on a wheel. You can only move or stop moving. And the only place you can arrive at by moving is somewhere else where you must either stop or move on.

Under the brittle ice my brain begins to stir and thaw. I have managed well on the surface. I like the ice. It holds me up. If I could have kept going – if I could go faster. If I could fly at the speed of light, travel on a rocket to outer space – then I'd be fine.

That's enough. Don't poke and prod me.

Story. An elderly woman. Not moving. Blocked and muffled in her life, immobilized. A musty spinster. An ageing daughter. Restrained. A pale drawing, not even pen and ink, I'll do it in pencil; a shadowy colourless stationary life.

The Spinster Daughter

Restraint. But. The clearest thing about her is the house. Kitchen painted bright gloss green and yellow. Should have been like buttercups, like daffodils, sunny. But the colours were too strong and the gloss too shiny, especially the green, and the room had the enclosed and sweaty air of a primary school cloakroom, a public changing-place. Gloss paint for walls is out of fashion now. And the curtains Alice Clough had made were a large and colourful floral print. The floor, of red quarry tiles, was fresh redded and polished every week, and glowed in the light of the brilliant fire which always burned – always, come summer come winter – in the kitchen grate. On the walls a variety of calendars, still supplied by agricultural merchants and purveyors of farm implements (despite the sale of the farmland back in the sixties), showed country scenes, smiling busty girls, and prize-winning shire horses. On the windowsills and sideboard stood orange and mauve gauze flower arrangements, which Alice had made following instructions in a monthly handicrafts magazine. The blanket that she had on the go at the time would be draped over a chair, with multi-coloured tails of wool dangling to the floor.

Where, in this hot bright little kitchen, is the restraint? Except in the form of the room itself. The windows were never opened; fresh air was poison to Alice's mother and could set her coughing for hours. Layers of cooking smells accumulated beneath the shiny cream ceiling, jostling for airspace: smells of boiling bones and baking custards, simmering jams and roasting potatoes. There was nothing dirty or old about this – the kitchen was spotless. It was just so hot; so full of things; so oppressive, that the milkman when he called to be paid on a cold morning was relieved to back out again into the frosty air, and the doctor rinsing his hands under the sparkling tap would say,

'The miners'll thank you for keeping them in work, Miss Clough,' with a nod towards the high-banked glowing fire.

Added to the heat and smells was frequently an element of steam, rising from sheets and towels draped over an old wooden clothes horse which stood with its arms out-stretched to the fire at night, like a large cold guest. The upper sections of the windows were often misted with vapour, and on Mondays the room would be totally enclosed, windows blinded with heavy condensation. Except that Alice would repeatedly clear a smear, at eye level, with her wet red hand, and peer out (at nothing) many times in the course of the day.

Alice Clough worked hard, in a small hot room, amongst garish colours, and was sustained by air that was saturated with smells and heavy with moisture, between gleaming dripping walls and opaque smeared windows.

They lived on the ground floor, she and her mother. Upstairs the house was decaying rapidly. The roof leaked, rafters were rotting, plaster was crumbling away and window panes rattled themselves loose and cracked. Lumps of Victorian furniture, furry with dust, stood in the shadows like stuffed bears. The electric did not work.

Downstairs Ellen had for bedroom the old parlour with its generous tiled fireplace and double window on to the garden. Her room was permanently semi-dark, shrouded from light and more pernicious draughts by heavy velvet curtains. The still air was warmed to oven heat by the ever-burning fire in her grate. Along the wall opposite her bed stood the old three-piece suite, upright but unused, waiting stiffly to resume its rightful position in the room. Alice's bedroom, a bathroom and scullery completed the downstairs, lived-in part of the house. The scullery, which was cold, was lined with her jams and pickles, and cluttered with broken furniture.

The state of the house was a reflection not only of Ellen's meanness but also of Alice's conviction that this state of affairs was temporary. There was no point in repairing the roof, renewing the windows, rewiring or replastering. Because soon Ellen would die, and Alice would sell the house. No point in throwing away good money on it. In fact Ellen's grip on her purse strings was so vice-like that Alice never had money, either good or bad, to throw at anything. When father died, he left everything to mother. When she died, it would be passed on to Alice and her brother Tom. Each would benefit in turn. And Alice waited her turn.

She had waited when she came back from her nursing in '45. Nursed her injured brother and said no to Jacko. She had waited while her father's health declined to invalid state, and waiting, had nursed him. Tom married and left home, and Ellen, suddenly deprived of both her menfolk, threw herself into illness with a determination that should have killed her within months. Alice waited, to nurse her. But Ellen did not die. She continued to be sufficiently ill to need constant nursing, regular doctor's visits, and a lion's share of sympathy, for twenty-five years.

Alice did not know it would be twenty-five years. That's the point about waiting. If you know it's going to be twenty-five years then you go away and do something else in the meantime. Alice lived the twenty-five years in daily expectation of the time being up. Every activity she embarked upon was temporary. Each decision was provisional. Her own life, 'for the time being', was in abeyance; her mother's demands were more justly pressing, for her mother was about to die.

Alice filled her time, while she was waiting. She nursed her mother with such skill and efficiency that the doctor complimented her regularly. Ellen was turned, and

31

washed, and exercised, and her diet so carefully adhered to, that she was almost entirely free from those secondary discomforts of long-term illness which cause so much distress. She never had a single bedsore, nor was she constipated, and she suffered from secondary infections only on very rare occasions. For years Alice forced her to get up for part of every day, just as she forced herself to cook twice a day – broths, custards, fresh vegetables in season. Ellen pointed out that she had no appetite – none – and that standing and moving was sheer torture to her aching bones. But she knew she owed it to Alice to make an effort, and she hoped Alice appreciated what it was costing her.

She had a hatred of light and fresh air, which Alice's training had taught her were great aids to healing. When Alice walked in and pulled back the heavy curtains, threw open the window and allowed the clean spring air into the sick-room, Ellen retreated beneath her blankets in paroxysms of coughing, afterwards tearfully accusing Alice of trying to kill her. Eventually Alice was forced to give up, knowing quite clearly that her mother was wrong, and also that her mother knew she was wrong. She believed Ellen took satisfaction not only in behaviour which would increase her own ill health, but also in bullying Alice into abandoning a practice she thought important. Making Alice give things up pleased Ellen. She thrived on it. As she thrived on sickness, and sickness on her.

Alice, growing older, grew bitter. It came on her slowly, as the concertina pressure of years of waiting accumulated behind her to squeeze her forward into a shortened future that could be her own.

Her own life had lasted three years. Until she was eighteen she lived at home with her family. Then (after a battle, but Tom had already gone off to fight and Ellen was so busy being devastated over that, that she didn't have much energy to spare for Alice) Alice joined a Voluntary

Aid Detachment and went south. She went with six other girls volunteering from the neighbourhood, to nurse convalescent troops.

The three years had had to last; the first magical exhausting year in the military hospital, and then her two years at Newcastle General doing her nursing training – broken off by the homecoming of her wounded brother. She had never thought she would still be feeding off those memories, thirty and forty years later. That nothing else at all would have happened. The memories, like old and retouched film, became oddly coloured, unreally bright. She was losing the sense that they had been her own life. As if it has happened to someone else. Another girl with chubby cheeks and long fair hair and a giggly, dimpling laugh. The most important memory, Jacko, had been subjected to so many viewings, so many touchings up, that she hardly knew it now. He was handsome. Kind. Funny. American. A hero; he had joined the British Army before the other Americans came into the war. It didn't last long – he was nearly better, and was going back to France. But they went for walks when she was off duty, and he kissed her in the fields. The afternoon before he left they lay down in the long grass; it was hot, he tried to – she was trembling, she nearly –

The poor film was so scratched and faded that she was no longer quite sure what had happened. What lingered like a smell was a nauseating sense of physical loss. Her fears had made her reject what her whole body craved.

She had been afraid of getting pregnant. Also afraid of seeming cheap, of losing Jacko. And perhaps she had been right there, because Jacko did care for her. He sent her five letters. And when the war was over he wrote to her from London, saying he was awaiting passage to the US. Could they meet? Tom was bedridden, the pain in his shattered leg still making him delirious from time to time. Alice braved her mother.

'I have to go to London.'

'To London? To London? What for?'

'I want to see – I need to talk to an American friend of mine – before he goes home.'

'An American?' Ellen said quietly. 'My God.'

'What?' cried Alice quickly. 'What's wrong with it?'

Ellen shook her head.

'Why shouldn't I go and see him? I love him. We might get married.'

Ellen snorted. 'That's what they all say.'

'It's true. Why shouldn't I go? I'm an adult, aren't I?'

'Yes.'

'Well?'

'Go. Go on. Go.'

'I – I was going to go and ask Mrs Munroe if she could give you a hand with Tom – while I'm away.'

'You needn't bother.'

'Look – you can't manage on your own, you know that.'

'We'll manage. If it's more important to you to go gallivanting off with a Yank than to look after your own flesh and blood that's nearly died fighting for your freedom, then we can manage, my girl. I've got some pride left, I hope. And I'll tell you something else, madam. If you go, you go for good. I'm not having you back here, after you've been off whoring down in London. You go – go on and enjoy yourself – never mind about your brother lying here sweating in pain. Never mind us. I just hope you can sleep nights, in years to come.'

Alice in her innocence saw time as elastic, able to stretch to encompass all good things. She wrote and explained to Jacko. She would see him when her brother was better. Perhaps Tom would come with her and visit him in the States! She would see him soon, and sent him kisses.

There was never time for her to go. And when she

became old enough to realize that she should go even though there wasn't time, it was too late. She looked grey and haggard. Jacko had probably forgotten her, married someone else. Besides, he never had, had he? Asked her to marry him. Only to see him. If she had gone then, she knew – she felt sure. But now it was too late.

Alice Clough was always busy. When she wasn't looking after her mother, or cleaning, or cooking, or washing or ironing, she would sit by the kitchen window, sewing or knitting. In summer she worked in the garden. She looked up at every set of footsteps coming along the little lane, and when she was inside she waved at every passerby she knew – milkman, postman, farmworker, farmwife. She knitted squares for blankets for the local old people's home. In season, she made pounds and pounds of jam to go to the church fête for charities overseas. Not that she was a churchgoer – she was needed at home too much for that sort of thing.

'Where have you been?' Ellen would call querulously, immediately, as Alice opened the front door.

'Just to the shops, mother.'

'I needed you and you weren't there.'

'What do you want, mother?'

'I was scared when I called for you. You should tell me when you're going out.'

'You were asleep.'

'I shouldn't be left on my own.'

'I can't stay in all the time. What would we eat?'

'You could have the delivery van.'

'He costs more. Besides, am I to be a complete prisoner?'

'I don't know what you mean.' Pause. 'How long d'you think it is since I last went out?'

'You can go out, mother – I'll take you out, any day. I'll set up a chair in the garden for you. It would do you good to breathe some fresh air.'

'You don't know how I feel – you've got no idea. You

can't have any notion of how I feel, or you wouldn't be able to talk about fresh air.'

'Well I'm sorry but I have to go out sometimes. You don't want me to get ill as well do you?'

'What a wicked thing to say. You should be ashamed of yourself. You go out – go out and enjoy yourself while you can. Don't think about me lying here on my own.'

'I don't go out and enjoy myself. I go out on errands to keep your house running. I go out to collect your prescriptions and buy your food. You won't be happy till I'm tied to the end of your bed, will you – till you've removed my last inch of freedom.'

Ellen starts to cry. 'I wish I was dead. I wish to God I was dead and with your father. Then I wouldn't have to endure this. What have I done to deserve this, God? Nothing but pain, whichever way I turn or look, nothing but pain waking or sleeping – and being told I'm a burden to my own flesh and blood. Dear God, haven't I suffered enough?'

Alice (calmly, bringing her a drink): 'Stop feeling sorry for yourself, it doesn't help.'

'I wish I was dead, I do. To think that I'm dependent on a selfish slip of a girl who resents every little thing she does for me and can think of nothing but blaming me for my sufferings . . .'

'Mother, I am not a slip of a girl. I'm a middle-aged woman. I do not blame you. I try to look after you. Will you stop it now?'

Ellen crying with increased force. 'Don't leave me, will you, Alice? Don't leave me. You're not going to put me into that home, are you? You're not going to leave me?'

The only way to cope was to be efficient. Do what needed doing – meticulously, everything. Be a machine. Alice woke in the mornings with lists of duties in her brain, and the list carried her from one task to the next, one hour to the next, day after day. The wheels went round, spoke after spoke. It was no use wanting anything else, or longing for it – she must go on steadily, day after day, boring on through time as patiently as a woodworm through a log.

In the winter of Alice's fifty-first year, she became ill herself. She caught a virulent strain of flu and was forced to take to her bed for three weeks. Dr Carter arranged for a home help and the district nurse to visit them daily. When she recovered, Alice was scared. She had been ill. She was getting old. She might die.

She might die before her mother. All this time waiting, all these chances given up, one by one: friends, romance, marriage, children, work, a career – and soon it would be her life. Soon she would have wasted her whole precious life waiting for her mother to die. She had never thought of death before. The very fact that it had yet to happen to her mother removed the possibility of it happening to herself.

But now she knew she could die. Why was there any reason to suppose Ellen wouldn't last for ever? She went on and on always against the odds. Dr Carter had told Alice it was a miracle.

'Still alive at seventy-nine, after all these years of illness? What a miracle! It's all thanks to your nursing, Miss Clough. A pity you couldn't have used those skills on a few more patients, eh?'

Staring fiercely out of the kitchen window, as the first of the spring hikers trudged up the lane to the Pennine Way at the top, Alice's eyes filled with tears. She had waited for it. Hadn't she earned it? Didn't she deserve it? Just one year – that's all – just one year to call her own, one year to live her own life in, before she must give it up. Hadn't she paid for it, in all those years she'd lived for others?

How to take it, how to grab it before it slithered on out of her grasp, was the question. How to catch that time and make it wait for her. In the first days of blind panic, sensing death's cold breath on her neck, she wanted to smash and run. Punch her fist through the smeary kitchen window and run screaming up the lane. Burst, like an overgrown chicken, out of the terrible confining shell of Ellen's house, and fling herself on the world.

Gradually she thought of a better way, driven continually by a strong sense of panic. She wasn't going to steal her time, or do anything wrong. She would save it. The time was hers and due to her; she would save it. She would do each day's task more swiftly and efficiently. Not by skimping or not cleaning in corners, but by working harder and quicker. So she would finish the washing and the morning cleaning by 11.30 instead of 12.30. Then they could have lunch. In the afternoon she would do the cooking and bathe her mother and weed the garden or whatever other chores she had to do, quickly – so that instead of finishing for tea at 5.30 she could finish at 4.30. But having already saved an hour in the morning, that would be 3.30. After tea her mother could be given her medicines and put to bed. Alice would wash up, do some ironing, do the darning and bake some bread – then she could go to bed, at 7.30 p.m. instead of 10. That day would be over. The next day could begin at 5 a.m., and on that day they could have their lunch at 9. That day would be over by mid-afternoon. And so on. Soon she was overtaking days, hustling her mother and herself through time with such exhausting efficiency that she was saving not just days but weeks. She would do next week's work this week, next month's next week – slide up the back of time and grab a year – a whole year of her life – for herself.

Ellen was poorly now. She rarely spoke, and spent most of her time dozing. The doctor really was astonished that she had lasted the winter. The old woman clung to life like a barnacle. It was no surprise to him that she gradually became comatose over that spring, and when Miss Clough asked for a repeat prescription four weeks early he assumed she had either dropped or mislaid her mother's tablets.

Alice, exhausted by her determination not to skimp on any of her self-appointed tasks, lived in trembling frenzy. There was a terrible underlining to the business of saving time, because it seemed to exhaust her (and so shorten her own possibility of surviving to enjoy it) more and more, each day she saved.

In April, the old lady died. Alice went in to turn her in the morning (it was in fact 2.30 a.m., and according to Alice's reckoning, a date several weeks after the actual one) and switched on the bedside lamp, as she usually did. She stirred up the fire and added fresh coal, before turning to her mother. As her fingers touched the wrinkled skin of the old woman's neck, she realized it was cold. Ice cold. Ellen must have been dead for hours. Her face was perfectly composed, as if she were still asleep; her hands rested neatly on the overturn of the sheet, like a doll in bed.

'Mother?'

It sounded odd. She had not spoken to her mother for weeks. There was no point. 'Mother.' She sat on the edge of the bed. The dead woman was small, she did not take up much space in the bed. Alice sat and stared at her.

She sat there for a long time, because when she finally stirred and went to the window, the darkness outside was lifting. Carefully, not making a noise, Alice pulled back the heavy curtains. A chill grey light filled the room, expanding it to twice its normal size. Alice stood uncertainly by the window for a minute then carefully closed the curtains again. The room folded in on itself, dark and reassuring.

Alice went quietly to the kitchen, and, sitting at the table, began to make a list of things to do.

Doctor.

Tom.

Vicar.

Undertaker.

Mother, wash and dress.

She was cold; she shivered and picked up the cup of tea on the table. But that was cold too. She'd made it when she got up at 2 a.m. Mechanically she put on her coat and set off for the phone box, shutting the front door silently behind her so as not to disturb the sleeper.

When she returned an hour later she went straight into Ellen's room. Her mother lay still. She was dead. Alice went back to the kitchen. It was cold. The fire had gone out. Moving slowly she boiled the kettle, filled a bowl with warm water and carried it to her mother's room. Carefully she stripped her mother's stiffening bird-boned body and rolled her on to a towel. She washed the familiar wrinkled flesh and dried her carefully. The skin was hard to dry. It wouldn't stop feeling cold and wet. Then she dressed her in her underclothes and a dress which Ellen hadn't worn for years. She rolled her over on to her back, and combed her hair. Then she spread a clean sheet over her. Ellen was ready. Ellen was dead.

Alice sat on the sofa opposite the bed. She would empty the dirty water in a minute.

She was sitting there still when Dr Carter arrived that afternoon. He greeted her kindly, offered her some sleeping pills, and enquired when her brother was coming. For the funeral, she replied, on Friday. Another doctor came in from the car to sign the certificate, then they both left. Alice went back to the kitchen and sat at the table. It was very cold. She would have got up to make a cup of tea, but it hardly seemed worth the bother.

In the night she roused herself from her chair, and hobbled into her mother's bedroom. The cold had sent her feet to sleep. Ellen was still there. She hadn't moved. She didn't need anything. There was nothing to do.

Alice returned to the kitchen. She switched on the light,

but the curtains had not been drawn and anyone could have seen in, from that blackness outside. She switched off the light again, steadying herself against the cold wall in the dark. Perhaps she should go to bed? But she couldn't remember what hours today was running to. And if she went to bed – when should she get up? And what do then? Ellen would not want changing, or giving a drink. The fire would not need making up. Nappies would not want soaking, nor sheets washing, nor food buying. There was nothing that needed doing. There was nothing for her to do.

When Tom arrived on Thursday night the house was in darkness. Alice must be in bed, but it was thoughtless of her not to leave a light on for him. The door was not locked but he tripped and hurt his gammy leg because he forgot the way the door sill stuck up out of the floor. The house was chilly. Rubbing his ankle irritably he switched on the light and called her. There was no reply. He went though the house room by room, switching on all the lights. His mother lay dead in her bed. In the kitchen he paced up and down, swinging his arms together for warmth, waiting for Alice to return. He'd had a four-hour journey, for God's sake. The grate was full of cold white ash. Angrily he riddled it, sending choking clouds of dust into the air, then laid and lit the kindling stacked in the fireside basket. The flames were reluctant and he spread a sheet of newspaper over the fire to draw it up. A fine bloody mess. Maddy might have come with him, instead of leaving him to sort it out all on his own; his mother dead, this filthy old ruin of a house, and Alice playing at silly buggers.

The roaring fire sucked in the paper and it blackened and burst into flames before he could let go of it. Shaking his hands in pain he stumbled back. A car drew up outside. Tom opened the door as Dr Carter came up the path.

'Mr Clough! Glad to see you. Is your sister here?'

'No. I don't know where the devil she is.'

Carter followed him into the kitchen. The fire had gone out again and the charred wood smoked sullenly.

'She phoned me,' the doctor said. 'About an hour ago. She sounded upset. I thought I'd come and see if she was all right. She's not on the way up from the phone.'

'I haven't even seen her.'

Carter nodded. 'She was saying that she'd killed Mrs Clough. Overdosed her with painkillers.'

Tom stared.

'There's no truth in it, of course,' the doctor said sharply. 'Your sister kept Mrs Clough alive for many years longer than she would have survived in hospital. She was an excellent nurse. Her reaction to your mother's death is one I should have predicted.' He paused. 'I blame myself.'

Tom rubbed his leg and tapped his feet, which were like blocks of ice. 'So what happens now? Where d'you think she's gone?'

The doctor shrugged. 'Probably wandering about. We'd best notify the police. My guess is she'll make her way back here, though.' The doctor moved back towards the door and grasped the handle.

'She'll get over it,' Tom said, not quite a question.

The doctor tested the door handle, as if he were about to repair it. 'In my experience, I doubt it. My guess is she'll follow your mother fairly quickly.'

The doctor and Tom stared at each other.

'Well, she could come and live with us. My wife used to be good friends with her,' said Tom defensively.

Dr Carter shook his head. 'This was her world, Mr Clough. It's like those Egyptian mummies that last for centuries in air-tight tombs. Perfectly preserved, centuries old, good as new. As soon as you open the door and let the

42

fresh air in they disintegrate – they simply fall apart.'

He opened the door and looked out into the black garden. 'I suppose you could say your mother did her a favour – lasting so long.'

When I thought of her – of Alice Clough, sitting in her kitchen, over the years, waiting for her mother to call her and complain – I thought she would long for children. But perhaps she wouldn't even have thought of it. Perhaps she was still so clearly, in her own eyes, her mother's child, that having children of her own did not occur to her? And then I thought, she must have wished she'd broken the rules. She must have thought all the rules so crazy and evil that there could be no reason for good behaviour left. Because if she'd done what she shouldn't have done, and made love with Jacko in the fields – then maybe she would have got pregnant, and maybe they would have been glad to let her go and marry him and have a life of her own. Or if Jacko had refused to marry her, and they'd turned her out – at least somehow, somewhere, she'd have had a life of her own, and a baby to love. Instead of nothing.

But I don't think she would ever have thought it didn't matter what she did. Or that it could have been right to grab what she wanted for herself. Did she really stay with Ellen all that time out of filial duty?

Yes. There was no question in her mind. Not out of love. She hated Ellen. But she knew what she ought to do. And she had never been taught it was a virtue to put your own needs first. She believed the opposite; that it was a vice, selfish.

Thur. 13

I have been lying in bed luxuriously smelling the sheets. I don't know how she's done it in February, but her sheets

44

smell as if they've been dried outside. They smell of sunshine.

'Lying in bed luxuriously.' I am outside the pale. A woman who has left her children.

My children have left me. Ruth and Vi have left me, and the twins aren't old enough to choose.

The twins need you.

No – the twins need someone. And they are of an age, and a cuteness, to arouse that protectiveness in anyone. The last person they need is me, mother of Ruth and Vi. 'Where's smother?' One of their giggly girly jokes.

That's enough.

Alice Clough. Trapped in that crushing routine of housework, the awful lists of tasks to be done and each day renewing them. Because we eat today doesn't mean we don't need to eat tomorrow. In fact not eating today could, eventually, be the solution to tomorrow – starve 'em long enough and they'll never eat again. (Does she make jokes, this woman who abandons children?)

She was set against it, and it wore her out. She hated the chores: soaking, washing, wringing, hanging up to dry; removing the clothes, stiff and bent from their positions on the clothes horse; folding, ironing, piling away. Cooking little messes of easily digestible slop, broth and scrambled eggs, and then the dishes to scour. Sweeping the floor and scrubbing the floor, disinfecting the bedpan, cleaning the toilet. Pushing back the tide of overwhelming dirt and chaos for a day, a week –

But now her efforts are forgotten. Her windows are streaked with dirt, mice and spiders scuttle in her cupboards, the heaps of freshly laundered clothes are rags. On dusty shelves there stand a few pots of fermenting jam. And the mouths that consumed the food are dead.

What if she'd taken pleasure in the scent of freshly laundered sheets? A woman taking pleasure in woman's work; preparing, preserving, waiting. Penelope and Sleeping Beauty, Cinderella, Ophelia, Snow White all waited: for rescue, for marriage, for their men to return from battles, adventures, and changing the world. Their virtues are passive: patience, chastity, fidelity. Waiting. We all wait. But in the waiting –

Alice sits in the garden top-and-tailing gooseberries to make jam for the summer fair. The sun is shining and her bare arms are hot. She itches her nose with her arm and feels the heat and smell of sun on skin. Her fingers touch the fat rounds of hairy gooseberry flesh. There is a heap of dark gooseberry tops like spiders and curved green tails the length of eyelashes, in the empty basket between her knees. To her left a half-full basket of red-green gooseberries; to her right, a shiny tin colander where the prepared fruit is mounting up. The farmer's wife comes up the lane and calls hello to her. She leans on the wall and asks after Ellen's health. They discuss the weather. She watches Alice and asks if she'll be making blackcurrant this year as well?

'That blackcurrant of yours I got last year was lovely. Too good for toast. I put a bit in a sponge cake with a layer of cream on top. Ooh, it was a treat.'

Alice's flying fingers finish the gooseberries; she leans back a moment, tilting her face up under the hot sun. Then scrambles up and takes her fruit into the kitchen. While the cold tap runs over the colanderful, she searches in the scullery for jars. Some are dusty; she fills the bowl with hot soapy water and washes them thoroughly. She leaves them to drain on the wooden draining board; tips the colanderful of gooseberries into the iron jam kettle. Puts the gas on low, adds a little water. As the gooseberries begin to soften, their strong sharp scent fills the air. She stirs, adds sugar, stirs. Looking out of the window she sees ox-eye daisies sway in the wind, the petals fall from a full-blown rose. She feels the grittiness of sugar dissolve beneath her stirring wooden spoon, and turns up the heat to boil her jam.

When she has finished twelve jars cool on the top shelf in the scullery. Twelve clear shining jars, each neatly topped with Cellophane sucked down in a taut semi-circle over the bright green jam; each labelled in black copper-plate on white: GOOSEBERRY August 1971. When she tips one the contents do not shift. It has set well. She steps back and counts the jars again, with satisfaction.

Yes. On that day and on other days. Satisfaction. Though the jam goes to the church fair where she may not go, and thence to breakfast tables across the parish where it may be left in preference for marmalade, or put away without the Cellophane and wasps get in it. No matter. She has made it and it's there, shining and green in bright sealed jars.

Satisfaction. In pegging out the washing between showers and having it dry before the next rain. Satisfaction running out as the sky darkens, to gather it into the basket and hurry back to the house, to shake and fold it in neat piles on the kitchen table: for Ruth, Vi, Gareth, me, airing cupboard. Satisfaction in its fresh-air smell, the rough texture of clean dry towels. Satisfaction in my airing cupboard piled high with clean sheets and blankets, extra bedclothes for visitors, outgrown clothes for jumble sales. The house and its order were mine. Gareth owned nothing, worked for nothing in our lives. Only himself, his advancement, and money. All the things that were washed and polished, grown and cherished, fed and cared for – children, garden, furniture, floors, the bricks and mortar that sheltered us from space – were mine. I made them, I loved them, I earned them.

But Ruth and Vi are not mine. They have chosen to go to Gareth. Away from me.

And for the tiles and furniture and chattels of the house – who wants them? The house is no more than a pit of work, an endless drain for labour. The floor is littered with the crusts and splatterings of food the twins have dropped.

It's indulgence, Marion. Everything was precious then. The gleam of a floor you no longer have the heart to sweep. Alice Clough can't have been unhappy always. Only in the story of her life, not in her days.

Fri. 14

A Nightmare

It's two in the morning, I'm sitting in bed with my jumper on. A nightmare. Devastated landscape. Hot sunshine. Flat empty grassland – to my left the ruins of a city, jumbled skyscrapers tilting at crazy angles, some snapped in half, with jutting broken edges against the skyline. Over to my right, near the horizon, the old dilapidated huts of a tribe – perhaps the original inhabitants of the plain. I thought South Africa. It was still and hot, a huge pregnant silence. I started to walk towards the ruined city, afraid of what I would find but not daring to stand there alone. I became aware of a noise, and very gradually – slowly, as if I were hearing in my sleep and couldn't wake up – I began to recognize the children's voices, Vi and Ruth shouting at me, and the twins crying, screaming in terror, at the tops of their voices. I ran towards the city as fast as I could, hurling myself across the level distanceless ground, running on the spot. Their voices were in the air all around me, resounding in my ears, and as I drew near to the first gigantic cracked wall, and saw the sun shimmering on glass and metal surfaces, I knew there was no one alive in the city. I spun round in terror, looking for them – by their cries, they were trapped and in pain. When I turned the cries grew louder, and I realized that all this time I had been running away from them. I started to

48

run back, through the hot still air; in the distance the grass and tin roofs of the huts shimmered in the heat, and the cries reverberated in the air so that I could feel them pounding my ears in waves. As I neared the village silence fell again. The cries had stopped. I ran into the deserted dusty place at the centre of the huts. All around me they stood silent, empty, doorways facing me. Some were half-collapsed, their corrugated tin roofs slipping drunkenly to one side. I ran into the largest hut. At the far end there was a low stool, and on top of it, balancing like an egg, a head. As I approached it I saw the eyes following me. It was Gareth. His eyes were moving. Though he had no body, he was alive. I must have cried out – I remember falling to my knees before him and staring into his face. There was no blood, no cut – his head was perfectly rounded at the base. I stared at him and then I put out my hand to touch the side of his face. His head rolled backwards and I jumped up quickly to save it from rolling off the stool. As I caught it, its eyes still watching me curiously, it came apart in my hands. In two perfect halves, like a chocolate easter egg. It was hollow inside. Perfectly clean and hollow, like an eggshell.

I was running across the grass landscape again, sweating and sobbing, with the renewed clamour of the children's voices rising up around me. There was nothing – flat grassland, not a bush or a hillock for a body to hide behind. And each way I turned, on all sides, the cries – 'Mummy! Mum! Help me, Mum' – and shrieks of fear and panic from the twins. My heart was hammering in my chest, my head was bursting. I crouched to examine the ground more carefully, then I started to look for them in the grass.

It was logical, for me to bend and hunt for them amongst blades of grass no more than two inches high. Indeed, as I searched, and the hot sun beat down on my neck, I was reminded of the time, years ago, that Ruth and

49

I spent an afternoon cricket-hunting. She noticed their whirring noise when I took her and Vi (still a sleeping baby in her pram) along a sun-hot lane in France on summer holiday, and I parted the grass at the roadside to search. As luck would have it, I uncovered one immediately, and we both stared in fascination as the little green insect rubbed his wings together in a blur of speed. Then he suddenly leapt out of sight. We parted more grass, and more – no luck. We walked on along the lane to a spot where their noise was particularly loud, and searched the grass again. But though we searched on and off for the rest of the afternoon, we didn't see another one – only heard their noise in the air all around us.

And so it was in my dream, only my useless searching in the hot sun was warped by a terrible anxiety, and my children's voices cried and pleaded and came and went in the air around my ears, above my head, in front of me and then behind me, imploring me to save them, to help them. Gradually as I searched I felt the dream slipping away, I was filled with anxiety, I couldn't remember what I was looking for or why. I couldn't remember what I had to do.

I managed to claw my way into wakefulness, and when I did, the beginning of the dream came back to me.

I shall leave the light on, as I try to go back to sleep.

Fri. 14, evening

It took me a long time to fall asleep again, and I woke with a jolt at quarter past nine. I felt anxious and confused, as if I had forgotten something or was late. My head ached badly. I needed to get moving as quickly as possible, to feel the smooth steering wheel turning in my hands and see the scenery slipping by. As I opened the front door the landlady called me back. I had forgotten to pay her. Standing at the desk trying to count out the money, I was afraid I might be sick; the floor and desk seemed to be moving slightly, as if on a sea swell, and I could not prevent myself from breathing quickly and shallowly. I needed to get into the car.

The woman moved slowly, looking in different boxes for change, talking lugubriously about the weather. I snatched my receipt from her and ran to the door without managing so much as a goodbye.

Outside it had snowed again, and the clouds looked heavy with more. I crossed the road to the car park on the other side, and for a moment I couldn't tell which was my car, under the layer of fresh snow. When I started the engine, the windscreen wipers wouldn't work – there was too much snow on the screen. My head was racing again as I got out. The cold made my fingers ache. I cleared the front and side windows – some snow got stuck under my cuffs and melted before I had time to get it out.

I revved the engine. Only a few cars had driven in the car park since last night – the snow in front of me was unmarked. But as the car started to move it went into a peculiar bumping motion. It would not steer straight. Already knowing the worst I got out and looked at it. The front left tyre was completely flat.

I had never changed a tyre, although I must have watched Gareth two or three times. I forced myself to look in the boot. There was a spare tyre, and a long plastic case containing a spanner, an iron rod, and a contraption which I took to be a jack. I lifted the tyre out and laid it beside the car. It sank to its full thickness in the snow. I began to scoop away the snow from around the flat wheel. A car slowly entered the car park, drove past me and stopped. A woman who got out came up to me.

'Are you having trouble?' I didn't reply. She bent over me and repeated her question insistently.

'No, it's all right. A flat tyre.'

'Oh, what a mess. Can I help at all?' I didn't reply. When

I turned to get the jack, I saw that she was crouching in the snow, fiddling with it. She set it beside me and knelt down to look under the car.

'Yes – you're better putting it under the front than the side, I think, with this sort of car.' She slid the jack under the front of the car and cranked it up. I stood watching her uselessly. Then she took off the hubcap and wheelnuts, removed the old tyre and put on the new one.

She knelt in the snow to force the new wheel on, and when she stood up I saw that there was a hole in her tights, and a little smear of blood where she must have cut herself through kneeling on a sharp stone.

'I'm so sorry – your knees –' I was not able to finish my sentence, and she stood awkwardly for a moment before slamming the boot on the old tyre and smiling at me.

'It's no trouble. I'm glad I was able to help. Goodbye now.' She walked quickly away across the car park, brushing her hands against her skirt as she walked, to dry them.

When I got into the car I burst into tears. It was a silly thing to cry about. She had been so kind. Helping me, kneeling down in the snow on her bare knees. I hadn't cried since I came away.

I've been ill.

She's brought me a paper. The date says I've been here five days now, it feels longer. Or – I don't know. Maybe not. It's been so fast and slow, so black and lurid, so hot and cold I can't really tell. She wanted to get the doctor in but apparently I told her I wouldn't see him. I told her it was only the flu, and not to bother him. I thought I'd said that, but then I remembered it as intending to but forgetting, so it stuck in my head as another irritation.

I don't know what else I said, perhaps not much; the woman, whose name I keep forgetting, is kind and a firm believer in sleep, so she has left me quite rightly to sweat it out.

I'm tired now, but over it, I think. My temperature's lower, I'm not hungry yet – even writing is an effort, pushing the pen across the paper. I feel weak – drifting, defences down. Open. I'll sleep again now.

Open.

When Ruth was being born, after I had lain in misery for seven hours, contracting without my cervix opening at all, the hospital shift changed and a new midwife came on. She was calm. Although she was efficient, she seemed to be giving only a fraction of her attention to what she was doing – the rest was absorbed elsewhere, in some great mind-expanding well of tranquillity. As if she could calmly have run the world and still had attention over to gaze at the stars. She examined me and said,

'You're fighting it. Go with it, stop fighting it. Let the pain do its work.'

At first I was angered – I was doing the best I could. As each new wave of pain rose and mounted I was clenching myself and resisting it, beating it off. I hadn't let it make me cry or call out, I had the upper hand. I was fighting the pain that was attacking my body: my muscles were tense against it, my spine was stiff to repel it. 'Relax,' she told me.

For a while, as I tried to relax, as I tried to imagine pain 'doing its work', pulling open clenched muscles, pushing back tight fearful walls of flesh to make space enough for a baby's head, I understood her. I knew what she meant by going with the pain; I allowed myself, briefly, to be open to it. I don't like pain. It is a hard thing to open yourself to. It is hard to surrender control.

But now I am here. It has all come roaring and tumbling about my ears. I thought, a great ball, like a planet, careering after me across the countryside. Now it has caught up with me it is a wave not a ball; a giant wave which has broken over me and engulfed me in a flood of memories and emotions, a swirling mass of flotsam and jetsam, days of my life. It is hard to surrender control.

The surf – on honeymoon with Gareth. We went down to the beach every day; the wet-suit-clad surfies had been out with their boards since dawn. The first morning I watched them with glee and imagined myself riding and swooping among them. Then I waded out into the sea. As I got to waist height I began to realize the size of those waves. They were breaking well before they reached me, but still the frothing torrent of broken water was half as high as me, and had the power to lift me off my feet and carry me backwards. Unbroken, what would the force of such a wave be? I swam on out with a mounting sense of exhilarated terror. There was a lull in the sea. I managed to get out quite some distance without meeting any big waves, only unbroken mounds of water not yet cresting, which I slipped up and down like a fast car on a humpbacked bridge. I was enjoying the cool freedom of the water. Then, looking ahead, I saw it. It looked as though the whole sea had gathered itself up, drawn itself together to make a giant vertical wall of water, which was racing towards me as fast as a train, blocking out the sky. I watched in terror. It was impossible to know whether to go back or forward. No way would I slide up this like a humpbacked bridge: already it was cresting at the top, frilled with a curl of white, gleaming teeth poised at the top of a giant jawbone which would come crashing, clamping down with the force of hundreds of tons behind it. It was as high, I think, as a house – a normal, two-storey house. It seemed as high as a block of flats, as it towered over me, and the crested white rim at the top curled over more swiftly, still suspended in air but caught in the pull of gravity. At the same moment the swell running before the wave lifted me towards the curling wall of water, and I realized that it would break, exactly, on top of me. That molten iceberg which hung in glassy suspension would break, the surface tension which held it together during its arched triumphant race towards the land would be overwhelmed by the sheer volume of water it had amassed, and that mountain of water would collapse, with the force of an avalanche, on my head.

I don't know how I came by the knowledge that saved me; whether I had been told it years before, and stored it unconsciously in the life-saving depths of my skull, or whether I worked it out on the spot; but as that wave hung timelessly over me, I took a huge breath and dived as deep as I could, into its base. Underwater, I heard the roar of its collapse, and felt the planes of water shifting and trembling around me. When my breath was used up and I fought out to the surface, it was gone, tearing away towards the beach in a seething, frothing, broken mass.

I did get caught by one later that day – not such a big

one. I underestimated it, thinking it was not quite going to break and that I could just slide up it. I slid up to its crest then the crest turned, curled, and dropped me to the depths. The water falling on me pummelled and pounded me and swirled me about at the bottom of the sea, bruising and scraping my shoulders and legs. It tumbled me over and over below the surface till I had no sense of which direction was up; the fine balancing channels of my head were awash and awhirl with salt water. It carried me up to the shallows, though, and from there I was able to crawl to dry land, stunned not to be drowned.

If I try to set it out, resolve it on paper – what form can it take?

Resolve.

It's a pleasing word, a good fit. Resolve; to find a new solution. Resolve; to dissolve the lumps and chunks that stick in my maw, to turn them to a sweet and palatable liquid. 'O! that this too too solid flesh would melt, thaw, and resolve itself into a dew.' Resolve me, then let me be resolved. What a beautiful, meaning-flowing word it is, how generously it encompasses all the hints and drifts of thinking I would like it to hold.

Be brave, melt, solve again.

It doesn't though, does it? Resolve.

Sweetheart, what is there to resolve? So much melodrama, this Marion, who does she think she is? What's her problem anyway?

You make me sick.

Leave. Time to sleep.

Fri. 21

I slept well last night. I think I have slept for most of the time I've been here, waking occasionally, feverishly, to have a drink and remember where I am, before dipping back under the surface of sleep, to be tumbled and rolled through time. I feel as if I'm travelling in my sleep, over landscapes where I have lived – through time as well as space. To talk of resolving is silly.

There is nothing to resolve. Nothing so concrete. Just images, some familiar, some forgotten. Just times, moods, impressions. An undigested life – a ragbag. It's all ordinary enough, except for leaving the children. Not many women do that.

What kind of a mother leaves her children? An inadequate, a selfish, an unfulfilled? Or a possessive, a demanding, a clinging, a smothering?

OK. I've stopped. I'm not running. I'm not hiding. I'm not David or Alice, I'm not in someone else's story, I'm in my life, and there won't be a resolution. There isn't the structure for it. It's not a story, it's a list of days.

All right. Make a list. It is after all the most sensible, housewifely thing to do. Make a list, tidy up. You can at least manage that, if not to resolve.

List

When Ruth was a baby, each new skill she mastered was a gigantic milestone. Sitting up, crawling, standing, walking: her first word. I crowed with delight when she did it, then I waited for Gareth to come home and see it. There is a flavour to that waiting that hangs in my head like a smell: the pride, the excitement, the determination that his pride and excitement should equal mine, the keen anxiety for the child to perform to order, the nagging sense that his smiles and applause may be feigned, that he may have preferred to have his tea first, that he'd rather have taken my word for it. My disappointment when she couldn't walk for him, didn't talk to him; my swallowed anger that both of them weren't behaving exactly as I wished them to.

And yet I was so happy, so proud, so loving. It lingers like a smell.

* * *

At night in their bedroom. I would go up during the evening to check on them sleeping, Ruth in her bed, Vi in her cot. Not just one but two of them, incomparably precious, sprawled carelessly under and over covers, limbs flung in abandonment, faces clean and sweet. When he was out in the evening (he never knew this, no one did) I sat by their beds and watched them sleep. Regularly – sometimes for an hour or so. I see their faces now in the dim light; the way Ruth often slept with her eyes not quite shut, her relaxed face as simple and sweet as a baby animal. She would move suddenly, as if impatient of my watching, and then become completely relaxed again, and roll back to her previous dent in the pillow. Vi slept on her belly, back hunched, bum in the air – face squashed sideways on the mattress. Sometimes watching through the bars of the cot I felt it was only my concentration that held her there, in life. I wondered why I should be so blest as to have her stay.

* * *

The first time I took Ruth swimming, she was eight months old. Everyone I passed smiled at her or said hello. I lowered her into the pool and she beamed at me – then I held her hands and pulled her through the water, and she began to scream with delight. Literally, she screamed, fierce loud screams of absolute excitement and delight. Her pleasure made me laugh so much I nearly fell over myself, and had to sit on the side with her till we both felt cold enough to be less hysterical.

* * *

Ruth at thirteen, going on a school trip to Stratford, couldn't decide what to wear. I was chopping onions, didn't look up as soon as she came into the kitchen – and when I did look, my eyes were watering. She stood aggressively in the doorway, looking suddenly older and also like someone else. I couldn't think who, till I realized she was wearing my favourite jumper, a black angora with a deep V-neck. She wore it with nothing underneath.

I told her she looked like a tart. I made her take it off.

She looked beautiful. It was my jumper. I didn't tell her she could try it on.

Now I don't wear it any more.

* * *

Gareth. Coming home and looking at me. Pressing me. And in answer I held up a child, talked of children, insisted that he share the revelling in children – myself hidden behind the wall of their achievements and demands, myself more secure than a nun in her cell, rung and hung about with children.

* * *

Gareth. As time passed, becoming the cipher that I lived with. The cipher of my creation, the cipher for whom I lived. In that bright innocent world when we were young and the children were young, that was the first worm, wasn't it, to insinuate itself to the heart of the rose?

It is hard to repossess the beautiful, absolute young Marion, in all her clarity of blinkered innocence. Not I, but she.

One spring evening, for instance. Gareth is working late (she has no idea. Where ignorance is bliss why should she want to be wise? She does not want to know him. She would not like him if she did) and she has put the children to bed. He is due home at nine. She tidies up, then prepares a meal, sets the table. She slips into the garden and gathers some flowers, arranges them on table and mantelpiece. Then she takes a bath and puts on pretty clothes, something she could not wear while the children were about. Preparing for Gareth's return.

Innocent Marion. Everything she does is for Gareth. She does not take pleasure in cooking, nor in eating the delicious food she has prepared; nor in the tranquil beauty of the home she has created. She does not enjoy lingering in the cool darkening garden, selecting long-stemmed pinks, breaking the twigs of fragrant orange-blossom. Nor does she wait for and take pleasure in the stillness of the house with sleeping children: the running bath and room filling with steam, the slow pouring of luxurious bath foam into the rushing water. She does not enjoy the sight of her own healthy body in silky, flattering garments, nor the feeling of her warm pampered flesh tingling with satisfaction and anticipation.

Oh no. She does it all for Gareth. And Gareth's interest and pleasure are her reward. In fact it was not even necessary for him to show interest and pleasure. He simply needed to exist, like a chair, to give meaning and purpose to all her actions, and to enable her to be happy. He didn't even need to speak. But if he should take himself away, when she is doing all this for him? She will be wronged, her joys ruined. And he will be guilty.

* * *

Vi accusing me. The night is clear, and the date, November 5th, the year before last. I was three months pregnant with the twins, feeling sick and slow. I remember I sat by the bedroom window in the dark watching the fires and distant rockets. There were patches of red sparks and that orange glow reflected in windows, of fires burning in gardens and on waste ground. In different areas of the sky there were spates of business, as different parties let off their rockets, their golden rain and shooting stars. I was out of it. We used to have a bonfire when the girls were little; now they were out together at Jackie's, Gareth was going to bring them home. I was at peace up there, with my precious bellyful, and the whole of London dark and lit up outside my window. Twice I heard the sirens of fire engines hurtling to fires that had got out of hand; their urgency accentuated my calm. I had no need to worry.

Then there was a flurry of noise in the hall, the door slamming, sharp breaths and footsteps running round the downstairs rooms. I sat and waited, part of me feeling that I was invisible, and invulnerable – the other part, paralysed with fear. The footsteps thudded upstairs – I recognized them.

'Vi?'

She came running, and stopped just inside the doorway. 'Mum?'

'Yes. What's the matter?'

'What are you doing? Why are you sitting in the dark?'

'I'm watching the fireworks. What's the matter? Where's Ruth?' Slowly she came over to me. As she approached the window the orange light from outside showed me that her face was blurry with smoke and tears.

'Where's Ruth?'

'She's OK. She's at Jackie's.'

'What's the matter then? Why have you come home on your own?' She stood hesitating in the darkness for a minute, then knelt down next to me. She was looking out of the window, at the fireworks. I began to stroke her hair. We both watched in silence for a little while. Her breaths quietened and I heard her swallow a lump down a couple of times.

'It's quiet here,' she said.

'Yes.'

'Don't you mind being on your own?'

'No. It's peaceful.'

'Where's Dad?'

'He's – well, I think he's at a meeting. He told me he'd pick you up from Jackie's but it's not ten yet, is it?'

'Mum! He's a liar –' She burst into noisy tears, shifting away from me to lean against the wall. 'He's a filthy beastly shit of a liar and I hate him!'

I let her cry for a while. To the south, an expensive party had got under way. They were letting off rockets four at a time, and each one fired – I counted – six coloured flares.

'Look. Isn't that pretty?' I reached for her in the dark and touched her cheek. She flinched away from me.

'Can't you hear what I'm saying, Mum? It's important.'

'I know.'

'What?'

'I know what you're going to tell me, Vi. That he wasn't at a meeting, or whatever it is you've discovered. I know all about it.'

'What do you know? What? WHAT?' She scrambled to her feet. She was shouting at me, and I felt my stomach turn over, although I knew I shouldn't be able to feel it yet.

'Don't shout. Go on then. Tell me what's upsetting you.'

She sat on the windowsill, her back to the outside, blocking my view of the fireworks. Her face was in shadow, I could see nothing but an occasional flicker of her eyes.

'Jackie ran out of butter for the jacket potatoes. I went down to the off-licence to get some. I was just walking along – I don't know – not even thinking – and I looked up and saw the car. Parked. Just parked in the row of cars lining the road, the back of our car, with Ruth's 'Save the whale' and my trainers I left on the window ledge. I just – I started – I went over to it to see if –'

I waited.

'Dad was in it. With someone.'

'Vi, it's all right. I know.'

'You don't know! They were –'

'I know, Vi. He's got a girlfriend. I know. It's all right.' I was feeling queasy, not balancing very well on my raft. I could hold out a hand to her, but I couldn't pull her out of the shocking cold water.

'What do you mean, you know? What do you mean?'

'Vi. Look, I'm sorry this has happened. It's stupid and careless of him. But it's not a major tragedy. It's not like you think.'

'You know about her?'

'Yes.'

'Don't you care?'

I might have laughed. If I did I shouldn't have done.

63

'Look, listen Vi. I'll try and explain it to you. It's something I – or Gareth – would have explained to you both, fairly soon anyway, now you're big enough to understand that no one is being hurt. OK? Will you listen?'

She snuffled, wiping her nose on the back of her hand. Behind her the sky seemed to throb as the flames leapt and dwindled in the darkness.

'It's hard for you, you'll understand it better as you get older. People – adults – don't stay the same. I mean, they change. You can be in love with someone and marry them and then find out a year later, or ten years later, that you don't love them at all.'

I had rehearsed it in my brain often and saying it was like lines in a play: I had no idea what it might mean to her, nor indeed what I meant by it.

'Are you going to get divorced?'

'Let me finish. No. Of course not.'

'Whose is it?' Pointing at my belly.

That shocked me. Then I was shocked, in my placid queasy invisible cow-bubble. When my daughter asked me if the baby I was carrying (the twins, had we both but known it) had the same father as herself.

'Gareth's of course. Stop interrupting me. You asked and I'll tell you – the least you can do is listen quietly. We changed all right? We were married, we had you both, we loved you both – we cared for each other, but still part of us had changed. You – you and Ruth – are the most important things to us. You know that, to both of us. But having said that – having put that first – there is still room – there has to be space for other things in our lives.'

'Do you?' she snapped.

'What?'

'Screw other people in the back of cars? Do you?'

I wanted to ask her if it was necessary to put it like that, but I didn't. 'No.'

'Have you got anyone? A boyfriend?'

'No.'

'Why not?'

'I don't want one, Vi, I'm perfectly content with life as it is – with you two, and now this baby's coming – I'm not interested in that.'

'But he is.'

'Yes, he is.'

'And you don't mind.'

'No.'

'You're married to someone and you don't mind them sleeping with someone else.'

'No, Vi, I don't. You'll understand it better when you're older. It's nothing to do with me, and it's not really anything to do with you. It's his private life, and as long as it doesn't impinge on us or hurt us, then . . .'

She was quiet, sitting on the windowsill, fingers clasping the ledge beneath her thighs, face bent forward into the shadow. I watched the sky. Up beyond the range of fireworks, a plane crossed, red landing lights flashing. I thought how many levels there are in the sky, it's like the sea turned upside-down. How much depth there is in everything. Being pregnant, the secrets of the universe were mine alone. I was less use to Vi than a stuffed dummy.

At last she said, quite quietly, 'You hypocrite.'

'What?'

'Hypocrite. You. Filthy lying hypocrite. You – both of you – how could you?' She was crying again and not every word was clear. 'How could you – all lies and lovey-dovey, even having a baby again – how could you be so disgusting – I hate you. I hate you – both of you –' She half-fell off the windowsill – I think she misjudged the distance – recovered herself, and ran out of the room. I heard her run along the landing and slam her bedroom door.

Outside a new shower of rockets burst into silver stars
with a distant pop-pop-pop.

* * *

The mural. When I was pregnant with Vi I thought, Ruth
will feel displaced by the new baby, especially because it
will sleep with us, while she must stay in a room on her own.

I decided to make her room nicer. On the wall opposite
her cot, I would paint a beautiful mural. I studied her
favourite book, nursery rhymes, and made drawings of
the things she liked best; the old woman who lived in a
shoe, and the cow jumping over the moon. I couldn't do
people so I made the old woman's shoe-house, with little
windows and blobs of children's heads staring out of
them. I spent evenings poring over the book and doing
rough drawings; when I had done my final drawing I
copied it on to graph paper and measured up squares on
the wall, so that I could transfer it accurately. I spent a long
time choosing colours and paints – emulsion wasn't
bright enough, and the tins were far too big. At last I got
something from a specialist art shop.

And then the work began. I painted while she was
asleep at nights. She was always a good sleeper. I brought
the Anglepoise from the desk, on an extension lead, and
aimed its illumination at the particular patch I was
working on. Sometimes the shadows were odd; sometimes I could see my dark, looming, pregnant shape
outlined against the squares, as if it too was waiting to be
filled in with colours. I was aware of her the whole time
peacefully sleeping behind me. I loved those evenings;
working quietly, watching the picture grow. The first
thing I filled in was the cow, a beautiful black and white

66

Friesian with bent forelegs and stiff straight hindlegs leaping for the moon like a rocket. Then the moon, fat and yellow as a wedge of Edam, lying on its back like a baby's cradle. When she woke in the mornings I would point out my last night's work to her, and she would clap and exclaim excitedly.

One night Gareth came home while I was still working on it, and said, 'Isn't that bad for her?'

'What?' I was filling in little green curtains at all the windows in the shoe-house.

'The fumes from that paint.'

'The window's open.'

'Yes, but it stinks in here, Marion. It can't be good for a child that age to be breathing in those fumes. Not to mention you.'

'All right. I'm stopping now.'

'Do you have to do it with her in the room?'

'What am I supposed to do – move her?'

'Why not? You could work in decent lighting then. You'll ruin your eyes.'

I could not be bothered to argue with him. He had no idea why I was doing it, why it was so important for it to be Ruth's room, that Ruth was in, while this magical wall grew. Any more than he knew that I worked on it night after night for weeks. He knew nothing. The fumes were negligible, I could hardly smell them.

'What do you think of it?'

'It's fine. Very nice.' He laughed. 'Marion my dear, there's been a technological revolution I should tell you about, though – you can buy posters these days, reproductions of great paintings. It's much quicker than doing your own. They're by real artists, too.'

I didn't laugh. He wasn't laughing either, because later that week he bought her a poster of that Chagall picture, the one of the cow and the moon, and he stuck it on the wall facing the end of her cot.

She liked it. She stuck it in her new room when we moved.

* * *

About the twins. With Gareth: 'I'm pregnant.'

'You what?'

'I'm pregnant.'

'Are you sure?'

'Yes.'

He laughed. 'That's all we need.'

'I want it.'

'Oh no – Marion, no.'

'Yes. Why not? It won't interfere with you, and the girls are practically independent now, it's not going to affect anyone but me – and I'd love it. I'd love to have a baby again.'

'You're fantasizing, Marion. You're thirty-eight. It won't be like it was before. Look, I don't want it. There's nothing to abortion these days, you can be in and out in an afternoon, honestly, it's less than having a tooth out. Marion, I must have some say in this. I do *not want it*.'

'And I do. You'd know all about the ease of obtaining abortions, I dare say. Spare me the blow-by-blow account of how much Carol enjoyed hers. I'm not your secretary, I'm not a little piece of fluff you can make orders about. It's mine. And I'll have it.'

'Over my dead body. And what about your so-called job? What happens to that?'

'It doesn't matter. I was going to leave. I can get paid maternity leave anyway.'

He grew more subtle. 'I know why you want it. Because you're too bloody scared and inadequate to form a relationship with another adult – you think a baby will solve all your problems. Mew mew mew, Mama Mama

Mama, you'll be meat and drink to it and the centre of its universe.'

'Why not? What's wrong with wanting a child to love?'

'You. You're wrong. You're perverted. There are enough children in the world, go out and love some of those, instead of making another one that never asked to be born.'

'Like you? Go out and love poor little eighteen-year-old girls, like you?'

And then he said, 'You needn't think you'll make me stay again.'

'What do you mean?' I hated speaking to him. I hated looking at him. When he spoke to me like that I was so filled with furious loathing the sight of him contaminated my eyes.

'I'm not falling for it again, Marion. If you decide to have it, you make that decision on the clear understanding that it is against my wishes, and that I want nothing to do with it. I've spent sixteen years doing your thing, being Daddy and mortgage and family home. I'm not doing it any longer. The girls are old enough now; if you have it, I'm leaving.'

'Leaving?' Why should I be surprised, why didn't I sing and dance and throw my hat in the air? I hated him.

'Yes, of course I am. We've done what we set out to do; we've lived in sodding wedded bliss, and managed to raise two relatively normal children. That's it. My part of the bargain fulfilled. At no place in any agreement we have ever made did it say the whole bloody business had to begin again after sixteen years.'

'No – indeed not. And of course you'll do something so different next time, won't you Gareth. You won't do anything as silly as live with poor Linda, or let her have the baby she's dying to have – you'll be rugged and independent, won't you –'

'Fuck off, you bitch.'

When he'd gone out I howled in rage, that I had said 'Leaving?' in that silly startled voice.

* * *

'What about your so-called job?'

It was always a so-called job. Never a real one. Even to me. It wasn't meant to be. OK, it was convenient – two and a half days a week when Vi started school, and I could drop them off and pick them up on my way to and from the big school, and have school holidays.

I never thought about that time. I didn't even think about it while I was there. A library assistant is invisible. I liked the peace and order, I suppose I enjoyed the mechanical, housewifely aspects of the work; the replacing in order on shelves, the retrieving and repairing of books. I never had to make any decisions about it. I just had to pad around quietly getting on with it. Then they sent me off one day a week to be trained, and Mabel had her hysterectomy, and didn't get any better, and I took over the reading and ordering, until gradually I was in charge, and the head introduced me to new members of staff and I had a budget. It still wasn't real, in comparison to Gareth's or Jackie's or the jobs I imagined myself doing when I did imagine it. It was too easy. Mabel used to flap when the first years came in in gaggles looking for books for their projects, or when fourth or fifth years had to be ejected for making too much noise, or eating. Then, I was glad I only had to tidy up books and put them away. But by the time I was Mabel they were easy to deal with, and if they weren't I fetched one of the deputy heads. It was ordered, the ground rules were clear. Sometimes I saw it as an island of peace in all the milling movement of the school. I liked it when it wasn't busy and I could go up to a child who was scanning the shelves with that glazed, hopeless look, and talk to him about something he might enjoy reading.

When I went into the staff room I was invisible. I talked to Janice, the lab technician. I ate my sandwiches and read a book. Teachers don't talk to librarians. It didn't matter – it didn't count. It was a so-called job, it had a wage, it was convenient for the time being. I was always about to apply for something interesting. Jackie kept bringing me the Creative and Media page with crosses scrawled on it; she could not see how absurd it would be, for me to try and get into anything like radio or TV. She thought Gareth would help me. It was the last thing either of us wanted; me, to be beholden to him, or him to have me around at work. It was impossible anyway, I'd been out too long. I'd done nothing. And I suppose it must be true, that I didn't really want to leave the library. Since I never did.

*   *   *

Ruth, in one of the school plays. She only had a tiny part, a messenger. A messenger ant, it was, in *The Insect Play*. She was twelve. When I saw her walk on to the stage I was furious. She was stiff with embarrassment, her thin shoulders hunched forward, her gait like a stiltwalker's. I knew what she really looked like. I knew how supple and agile her body was, how graceful her movements. Now, on display before an audience, she was laughable. I was angry with the stupid man who had directed the play, for not telling her to move differently. But I was even more angry with Ruth – who had a beautiful, flowing body and nothing in the world to be ashamed of or embarrassed by. I wanted to shake her and tell her not to be so stupid. I wanted the world to see her as I did, I didn't understand why she had to be so stupid and obstinate as to want to hide it. I told her afterwards, how ridiculous she'd looked.

71

Ruth. At the beginning. When I told her I was pregnant.

It's sixteen years since I had her. She can have babies too now. Suddenly weak and evasive, as if she's the mother and I the daughter: 'I've got something to tell you.'

Uninviting silence.

'Well, I'm pregnant.'

'At your age?' She's flat, hard, incredulous. 'You must be mad.' She's standing up, as if impatient, as if she wants to leave the room. 'What are you going to do with a baby?'

I try to laugh. 'Look after it, I suppose, bring it up.'

'Well, you needn't think I'll look after it for you.'

'I didn't think anything of the sort, although I did think you might be slightly more gracious and welcoming.'

Sullen silence, lips pursed. She's pushing a paperclip across the carpet with her toe. 'You'll have to stop work.'

'Yes.'

'Did you plan it?'

I'm watching her. She won't meet my eye. She hardly ever does, these days. If I don't tell the truth, Gareth will. 'No.'

'It's an accident?'

'Yes.'

'Why don't you have an abortion?'

It's what I would say to her, of course. 'Why should I? I'm perfectly healthy, we can afford to look after a baby, I like children – I'm glad I'm pregnant. It's an accident that pleases me, what possible excuse could there be for taking its life?'

'You've had your family. You've been a mother.'

'That doesn't mean I have to stop, even though you'd clearly be delighted to disown me.'

She never looks at me. Kicking and scuffing at that

72

wretched paperclip. 'I think you're making a mistake,' she announces.

'I don't care what you think, you are the most completely self-centred person I've ever met,' I cry childishly.

'You made me,' she tells me calmly, before going out and closing the door very quietly. I pick up the paperclip.

* * *

The first day it moved. The baby. I didn't know there were two, yet. In the kitchen, about nine in the evening. They'd all been there for dinner. Gareth left straight after to go back to work or to Linda's, I forget which he told me or which was true. Ruth was going to a school disco and we'd had a row about when she should be back by. Gareth didn't want to be tied to picking her up (so it probably was work, in fact) and said she must get the bus. Vi went to do her homework with Helen at Jackie's, and would probably stay the night but would ring me. I had cooked them ratatouille, I'd used olive oil and the heavy taste of the oil made me queasy. I sat and chewed dry bread and watched them eating. Then they all went out and left me with the swimming plates, tomato pips and bread crusts, crumbs of a French loaf all over the floor. I was very tired and the kitchen was a mess. I got up at last and stood at the sink, turned the tap on. As I straightened myself I suddenly felt it move – the touch of the child inside me. It was like a torch – God, I was so glad. I was so glad that there was a baby of my own in my belly tapping me to tell me she was there.

* * *

When they were babies I was so happy. Ruth and Vi. Now I look back I can hardly believe it was me. Sitting on the sofa with Vi on my breast, her little monkey-skull still visible through the down of black hair, her hands slowly clawing at my blouse in pleasure as she sucked; Ruth, big and grown-up and serious, all of two and a half, sitting beside me holding the book, while I read her a story and told her when to turn the pages. The sweetness and order of our lives, like 'a box where sweets compacted lie', each pleasure clear and distinct.

Their bath time. When I'd tested the water with its creamy layer of bubbles, I'd lift Ruth in; Vi lying kicking and gurgling on the changing mat on the floor. Ruth would stand for a minute, enjoying the warmth of the water, her little round tummy sticking out and her back deliciously hollow.

'Sit down, Ruthie.' Slowly, she would sit, dipping her hands in and out of the bubbles – raising them, watching the bubbles drip from her finger ends – looking up at me and smiling. Then she would turn and kneel up – ceremoniously, one by one, the toys would be lifted down into the bath. I can see them all, the first set of bath toys – the dented yellow duck and her two ducklings, the squashy sponge ball that used to squeak, the jug and the floating frog with squinting eyes. Before Vi was born we had a stack of yogurt pots too, some with holes pierced in to make sprinklers. But Ruth and I decided it might be too crowded for the baby. On the radiator their pyjamas, Vi's nappy and sleeping suit, and two towels were warming. Ranged on the shelf, just within arm's reach, were powder, Vaseline, nappy liners, pins, cream, shampoo, hairbrush. I lowered Vi into the bath slowly, while Ruth scooped her toys back out of the way. When Vi was submerged, and I was supporting her head and neck with my right hand, her little limbs floated in the water, and she wriggled them in sensuous pleasure. Ruth poured water for her, and gathered up the bubbles, and Vi laughed aloud to see her. I remember the round smooth texture of her baby skin, rubbing her body with my hand, running my forefinger along the crease at the top of each chubby little thigh, swooshing bubbles over her tummy. Then reaching behind me with one hand (the other supporting her still in the water) to grab the warm towel and spread it over my knees; lifting her, skinny and naked as a fish, on to my lap and wrapping her round: the tiny, brilliant, vivid life of her. When she was dry and lying on her back on the changing mat, I'd kneel over her – lower my head slowly towards her. Her eyes would widen and widen as our noses drew closer – nearly touched – and at the last minute she would burst out laughing, reaching up for my hair with her little starfish hands. When her top was on I'd leave her to kick, and wash Ruth, who'd been swimming and sliding up and down, scolding the ducks, bombing with the soggy sponge ball. I dried her on my knee. She was heavy and solid, in no danger of melting away now, solid and dear to my heart. I tickled her until she could hardly breathe for giggling, and gave her great raspberry-blowing kisses on her tummy and her arms, while she wriggled and shrieked and clung on to my knees. How gigglingly sweetly they went to bed – Vi turning and curling into sleep the instant her thumb was posted into her mouth; Ruth cuddling beside me for her story and glad to snuggle down under the blankets afterwards, tired and happy, welcoming sleep.

Days of order, days of grace, days of measured contentment. I thought they would come again. Days that I could control.

* * *

Days that I could control. The worst and blackest day, when I had to leave them. Gareth's ultimatum; you will come away with me for a weekend, you will leave Ruth and Vi with your mother. We haven't had a single night without them since Ruth was born – it's ridiculous. They're not the only people in the world, you know.

He was jealous. Once I recognized this I despised him for it. How typical of a man to be jealous of his children, instead of lavishing all love upon them and basking in the tenfold warmth they return. How silly and possessive of him to insist on his wife's individual attention.

But having said that the children would miss us, would keep Mum awake at night, would be unsettled – what other reason or excuse could I give for not going? To say I couldn't bear to leave them for forty-eight hours would have sounded ridiculous, even to my ears.

He booked a hotel in the Cotswolds. I began to pray that they would be ill, so I couldn't leave them. Vi was just weaned, she must have been nine months. I lay awake at night agonizing about it. I had never left them, not for so much as an afternoon – except for leaving Ruth while I gave birth to Viola – and she was excited enough about the idea of the new baby not to be too upset by that. The contortion in my brain, of course, was that it was entirely ludicrous not to want to go; that I was pathetic, laughable. Where was my healthy selfishness?

It was in loving my children. Selfishly, I wanted to be with them. If Gareth had offered to go away on his own I would have been thoroughly relieved. I was ashamed. I talked enthusiastically about all the things we would do during our great escape; about the luxury of not being woken at 4 a.m., about the joys of an uninterrupted dinner. And in Gareth's every word of eager anticipation I saw betrayal of the children, how little he cared for them.

During the week before, I shopped as if preparing for a siege: bought stocks of disposable nappies and baby bubble bath, then new pins and plastic pants in case Mum couldn't do disposables, jars of juice and first-stage baby goo for Vi, sweets and treats and special colouring books to keep Ruth happy. I washed and ironed every article of clothing they possessed, while they ran about in old and outgrown garments; I bought a set of new bottles for Vi so that I could leave enough sterilized for the whole weekend. I agonized over which toys to pack, I planned and foresaw needs and dangers until my head ached with the pressure.

They were both healthy. My mother was looking forward to having them. On Friday morning there was no escape. I knew from the terror in my mind and the looseness in my bowels that if I left them they would almost certainly die. And yet I was going to leave them. Because I was too ashamed of myself to stand up to Gareth and tell him I didn't want to go. By my own actions I was bringing catastrophe on myself.

At lunchtime I bundled a packet of nappies and a change of clothes each into a plastic bag, put it and the children in the car, took them round and unceremoniously dumped them on Mum. I left without kissing them goodbye. I ran back to the car and went to collect Gareth from work, so we could set off early on our wonderful second honeymoon weekend. Since leaving them was tantamount to condemning them to death, what hypocrisy to pretend concern, and ease my conscience with provision of bubble bath, favourite toys, and puréed beef broth.

That was the first, and the worst. But I never learnt to leave them graciously. I could never bear it. I always had to dump them and run.

What sort of a mother?

* * *

Sun. 23

And more recently, Marion? On the more recent occasion of you leaving your children, your younger children, your baby twins – did you make any provision for their welfare in your absence?

It was not the same. And I did make provision. Sensible Sarah was in the bath, the twins sleeping in their cots. After her bath she would come down to watch News at Ten with me, and find my note and the money on the kitchen table. She came from Edinburgh to help me with the twins; she had come to shoulder the very responsibility I left her with. The babies are not abandoned, they are left with a responsible aunt, better able to care for them and look after them than I.

I try to imagine them and I can't. I try to imagine them crying, but I can't see their faces – or decide which one I'd be looking at. I try to confront the damage I may have done to them; the gaping insecurity opened up under their scarcely balancing baby feet. I consider how I may have scarred the new lives entrusted to me.

But I hardly can. They are shadowy. I have never been able to see them. And by leaving them, I relinquished control.

With Ruth and Vi I couldn't bear to. It was like handing over control of my own body, letting someone else eat and sleep and breathe for me. I knew how to do every little thing for them, down to the smallest detail; how they should be got up and washed in the morning, how potted and dressed, how breakfasted and groomed. Each detail of their daily routine was as clear in my head as my own, and the notion of someone else doing it – of any of it being done differently – appalled me. I remember Sunday mornings when Gareth offered me a lie-in, and I lay fretfully in bed listening to him forgetting to clean their teeth and not knowing which drawer the clean socks were in, until I came to dread Sunday more than any other day of the week. Once or twice I stupidly got up and barged in to help. He was furious.

I controlled them. I owned them. Their attention was

mine to dispose. How I showed them – everything. Look at the doggy / horse / pretty flower / trees in the wind / sun on the sea / boy in the book / girl on the bicycle. Listen to the fire engine, burglar-alarm, ice-cream van. Smell the roses, shoe polish, niffy cheese. Look listen learn say; they were mine to give the world to and the world was mine to give them.

When Ruth was three I took her to a mothers and toddlers group. Vi was asleep in her pram. It was raining, and the church annexe we were in echoed with the pattering of rain on roof and windows; was full of the smells of floor polish and damp hair and old wood. For the first ten minutes Ruth clung to my knees, then gradually she became interested in the toys in the hall. There were small bikes and dolls' prams, a wooden climbing frame and slide. I watched her investigate the climbing frame; standing staring at the children on it, then plucking up courage to test it with an arm and a foot. I was bursting with pride – she looked so compact and perfect, held her back so beautifully straight, and gazed with such absorbed interest at the world around her – I couldn't help thinking she must be a magnet for all attention in the room. As I watched her wander from toy to toy – always slightly wary of the other children, slightly reserved, exploring – the pride and pleasure I took in her swelled to bursting point and I could hardly stop myself from crying. She was on her own there. Following her own interests, having her attention caught by varying objects and incidents, undirected by me. That sense of her as separate – and yet as connected to me as my own limbs – was unbearably poignant. Like being in love, yes, piercing like being in love, and seeing the other person so magical so beautiful so perfectly close to your heart's desire – and so separate. So able to walk away, at any time.

Because I was in love with Gareth and had that heart-rending sense of his separateness from me, I married him. It's why grandparents have their dressers clogged with photographs of babies and weddings. Real children grow up, real marriages crumble.

A story.

What Sort of a Mother

He's sleeping. His quick shallow breaths fill the air like fluttering insects above the bed. She always leaves the lamp on till she comes to bed, because he's scared of the dark. Standing by the bed she looks down at him. His face is tilted up on the pillow, his lips parted to suck in the air. His big face is like a baby's.

The fat woman undresses methodically, padding quietly about the room. She pulls on a long flannel nightdress. She likes getting in bed with him. He's hot. Not sweaty: hot and dry as an oven-baked potato, with smooth skin. He sleeps deep; doesn't even stir when she crawls in beside him. His quick breaths just raise his ribs beneath her arm. As she settles and quietens, she falls into the old pattern, one breath to two of his, one breath to two of his. To the rhythmic pull of their joint breaths she launches out into his sea of sleep.

She's never slept so well as with him. The others came in bed when they were little, but they tossed and turned, or pulled her hair. When they were babies she'd fall asleep slumped over Donna or Wayne or Tracey on her tit and force herself awake in a panic, scared to death she'd smothered them: find them curled like fat little leeches further down the bed, and her half-full tit still dripping for them.

And men – none of them was so good, for sleeping. Men were noisy and smelt bad; snoring and farting, turning their bulks in stiff heavy movements that jarred her sleep, knocking against her – foreign bodies. Their breath stank. Gary turned and flowed with her like he was still part of her own body – abandoned and floppy in his sleep as a little child. The sun-heat of him pervaded her aching, work-horse body.

The woman in the dock was short and puffy with ill-health. She also smelt badly – mixed body and vegetable odours – sweat, stale urine, cooking fat, and a sourish tang familiar to the escorting warders: fear.

Leonie Doyle. Forty-one. Mother of six. From flat 213, Christie's Tower, Blackhill Estate. Charged with the murder of her youngest son. She watched the court with a stupid, vacant expression, and had to be asked several questions twice. The medical report stated that she was of average intelligence, but suffering from severe depression. It was at this early stage in the trial that the murder charge was dropped, and replaced with a charge of manslaughter by reason of diminished responsibility. In court she never spoke more than five words together; in the safety of a cell, she talked freely to her social worker, whom she had known for fourteen years.

Leonie Doyle had lived on Blackhill Estate since it was built in 1961. She had been seven months gone with Donna, when they offered her and Des a twelfth-floor flat. Ten years later she was living in a bigger, fifth-floor flat, with her six kids and no Des. Good riddance, as far as Leonie was concerned. He was rough when he'd been drinking, and one time he broke her arm. That was when she was expecting Gary, the youngest. A few months after the kid was born he left. The Social traced him to Blackpool, trying to get maintenance out of him, but then even they lost track of him. He never had any money anyway. He drank it all. She was better off without him.

Her babies were all born perfect. Not even a birthmark on them, she was proud of that. Gary didn't get ill till he was nearly one.

Something's wrong. It's light. It shouldn't be light. He's never slept through – till eight o'clock? No. They're yelling and screaming next door, enough to wake the dead. That's how it starts, I remember. He's lying in the bottom of his cot, lips

blue, back arched. It's that what woke me, not the screaming,
the light. And that little gasp of his. His eyes're rolled up till
the pupils're nearly out of sight. I'm fumbling, letting the
cotside down, quick, reaching for him – he moves. He's
curling. Crisping. Like a strip of bacon under the grill.
I'll never not see that again. Crisping. When I wake nights I
see it. I see it when I look in his face sometimes. His little body
crisping with pain. Don't talk to me about God.

Unlike many babies, Gary did not die from the acute
meningitis he suffered at the age of eleven months. The
infection responded to treatment, and after three weeks
Leonie was told she could fetch him home. She had to take
Darren and Tracey (the others were at school) and they ran
around the consultant's room screaming, while he explained to Leonie that Gary had suffered a certain amount
of irreversible brain damage, due to lack of oxygen during
the convulsions.

He's a little baby again now. His mouth's gone slack, he's
dribbling again. He's no more better than I am, he's going
backwards. He was crawling three months ago. Look at him
now. As if I haven't got enough to do. And he feels different.
Heavier; he's not helping himself. Poor little sod. It'd be better
if he'd've died.

Gradually she stopped noticing the difference. He was
just the youngest – always, by a long way, the youngest.
When they started taking him to that special school by taxi
it was all right; for the first time, they were all off her
hands during the day. There was time to sweep the floor,
wash up, stuff a couple of bin liners with dirty washing
and set off for the launderette where there were other
women to talk to, and no sense of guilt in taking the
weight off her feet for an hour while the wet clothes

slopped round and round in a grey froth on the other side of the thick glass.

Days and nights and days and nights of them getting older, getting out from underfoot. Fewer of them in her bed at night, though no extra sleep because they still fought morning, noon and night, scrapping and yelling and breaking the furniture, shrieking and giggling in their bedrooms till the small hours – or out with the other kids, running up and down the walkways and dropping things off, trapping each other in the lifts, getting stoned on glue and cider, fighting. They ran wild. She didn't want them to, didn't intend it – but there were too many of them, and as each one grew older she stopped being the person that mattered and became simply the drudge – the one that brought food into the flat that could be taken from the cupboard, fridge or table, the one that locked the door at night and paid the telly man and the club for clothes. She simply was the flat – a place to hide or sleep. And she was money, either by asking or by theft.

Gary was the only one who didn't get older. Didn't stop needing her. Didn't stop smiling at her and hugging her and creeping into her bed at night. When it got to the stage of them all being out with the gangs of other kids on the estate, she and Gary had the flat to themselves. She'd cook a tea for him and herself – the others came and went as they pleased, grabbing food when they fancied it or begging money for pies and chips.

She and Gary would eat sausage butties in front of the telly; he would help her to dry up, carrying cups one at a time from the table to the cupboard, performing each task with the careful interest of a child. He would talk about his day at school, the teachers and the story he'd been read; bring home misshapen drawings of people with huge heads and stick bodies, as the others had done when they were little, before school became a dirty word.

He's a good boy. He loves his Mum. I tell him he can make us a cup of tea. He fills the kettle, with the tap running slowly, watching it, careful. Turns the tap off before he moves the kettle out from under it. No splashing. Checks the switch is off; plugs it in. It always takes a bit longer than you think, it's like he's the other side of glass — or water. I think sometimes, he's just putting his hand through, he's just putting his eyes through. When it's plugged in he switches it on. Waits, till he can hear the noise of the element heating. Then he gives us a smile. He's got a lovely smile. He's so busy smiling he's forgot what's next so I point to the mugs. He puts them there side by side. Pushes them carefully a couple more inches back from the edge, like he's arranging them for a bleeding display. Every little thing matters to him. I like watching him, when I'm not in a hurry. It's soothing, like watching them fish at the dentist's.

Only he's not like the fish cos I know what he's doing, I know why. He pushed the mugs in from the edge so's they won't fall off; he puts a tea bag in each cup, and when he's put them in he has another look to make sure they're in. When the kettle boils he watches it till it switches itself off — I've told him not to touch it, it'll boil for a good minute before it goes off though. Then he pulls out the plug, holding the handle of the kettle as if it'll bite him, turns it round awkwardly so's he can grasp it with his right, lifts it slowly and pours into each cup. He never spills a drop. When he puts it down he gives me a look again, checking I'm watching. Then he squashes the bags with a spoon, he likes that bit, sometimes he starts to hum to himself. He does what I've told him — pulls a saucer by the cup, fishes the bag out, drops it on the saucer. Then the other cup. Then he's getting the milk out the fridge — carrying it carefully, with both hands, taking the top off careful, careful, with his big clumsy fingers.

It can take him fifteen minutes to mash a cup of tea, I'm not kidding. But he'll do it. And be pleased as punch, when at last he's coming towards me carrying the mug high, not a drop spilt — grinning from ear to ear.

I know every movement. Every move he does, I know. Like I made him. I tell him how to do it. And when they learn him something new at school he comes home and shows me; he can write his name. When he does something wrong, I tell him. He doesn't get let off. He learns from it.

She tried to keep up with the others. Scolded Tracey and locked her in after the first time she stayed out all night. Went down the school to see the teacher when she got a letter about Wayne truanting. Had long talks with Donna and took her to the doctor's herself to get her put on the Pill, when she started going with that Damon. But if she locked them in they simply went sullen and silent, pretending to ignore it when she unlocked the door again, then walked out past her as if she was nothing – dirt. It was all battle, with all of them; a losing battle, as she well knew. When she controlled one side of her family it went tearing and roaring away like a forest fire in every other direction.

All except for Gary. He loved her. He wanted her. He was hers to control. If she was cross with him, he cried. When the others were in she had her work cut out protecting him, and he clung to her side. If they teased or hurt him it could rouse her to slapping them still, big as they were. When the girls suddenly took a new interest in him and invited him into their room for a lot of whispering and giggling she knew damn well what was going on, and called him out. She slapped him and shut him in her bedroom, then went to deal with a sniggering Donna and Lynda, and a quiet sulky-looking Tracey.

'You leave him alone. You hear me? He's a little kid. I know he's big – but in his mind he's no more than a little boy just starting infants'. Just keep your nasty ideas to yourself and don't go mucking about with him. You hear me?' She slammed the door on them and after a couple of minutes they trooped out sheepishly and went off outside.

She listened to him crying and throwing himself against the bedroom door. He'd be all right. No one was going to get away with hurting *him*.

After the initial terror and howling, he slumped against the bedroom door, sobbing heartbrokenly. She lit a cigarette and sat at the kitchen table listening as his cries tailed off then restarted with a second wind. He was crying mechanically, perhaps having forgotten why he'd started.

'Shut it, you thick pillock!' she shouted. 'You retard!' She would look after him. If she had ever heard of him being upset at school she'd have been down there within the hour, ready to do battle. But if she made him cry – as long as she was listening to him – he was all right. She knew she meant him to be all right. It didn't count.

And then she met Bill. The council were finally getting round to decorating the flats. Leonie's kitchen and bathroom were ruined with condensation. Bill and his mate Ted started work in the kitchen one April morning at 9. Leonie cleared stuff out for them, then went off to do the shopping. When she returned, Bill was on his own. She made them both a cup of tea. He stared at her in silence until she felt uncomfortable.

'Where's your mate?'

Bill laughed.

'Go on.'

'Two floors down.'

'I thought you were all finished down there.'

'Yeh – well. He has a little job down there that keeps needing a bit of touching up.'

Leonie stared at him blankly. Bill raised his eyebrows, then shrugged, and returned to his tin of paint.

Putting clothes away in the bedroom, Leonie realized

what he'd meant. Sitting down heavily on the bed she imagined the workman, in the flat two floors below, taking off his overalls and watching the woman as she unbuttoned her dress. Leonie had not imagined such a thing for a long time. Moving slowly, she went to the bedroom door and opened it a crack. She could see, through the half-open kitchen door, the painter's shoulder and arm pushing the roller rhythmically up and down, covering the wall by the sink with white paint. Hypnotized, she moved into the corridor and along to the kitchen doorway, where she stood still, staring at him. Eventually he turned and saw her.

'What's the matter?' he asked sharply, angry that she had made him jump.

Leonie didn't answer.

'What's the matter?' he shouted, approaching the blank-faced woman in the doorway. 'Have you lost your bloody tongue?' Something in her attitude and her silence filled him with blinding rage and he grasped her roughly to shake her. Unbalanced, she swayed heavily against him, and he saved her from falling by pushing at her other shoulder with the hand holding the paint roller. It clattered to the floor, splashing them both with paint.

'You stupid bitch! What the fuck's the matter with you?' He was propping her up, hands pushing against her shoulders. When she still didn't speak he gave her a slight push, and she bumped back against the wall.

'What? What? What d'you want?'

With a grotesque movement, her head and shoulders lolling against the wall, her hips suddenly jutted forward. He moved quickly, pushing her back against the wall with the weight of his own body.

'You want that? D'you want that? A fat ugly cow like you?' He ground himself against her, and she began to press her crotch rhythmically to him. Her plump face, slightly upturned to him, was still expressionless. Raising his right hand he slapped her across the cheek, while their hips continued to press and gind rhythmically. They both climaxed quickly, pressed against the wall, fully clothed. When he stepped back from her Leonie slid down and slumped on the floor.

'You dirty bitch. Look what you've made me do.'

She watched him dully as he pulled open his overalls and wiped himself on a tea-towel he'd picked up from the kitchen floor.

'Filth, you,' he said; picked up his roller, and continued with his painting.

It was like a drug. While he was still painting her flat they did it two or three times a day, while he hit her and abused her. Leonie moved about her life in a stupor. She had never experienced such a thing before: hadn't touched a man, or wanted to, for years. When he moved on to other flats he returned to hers at least once a day; when the children were out she sat, almost paralysed with longing, waiting for him on a kitchen chair, her body beginning to tremble and jerk at the first sound of his voice in greeting,

'Well, you filthy bitch – what're you waiting for?'

Lynda one evening noticed the bruising on her mother's face, and asked what she'd been doing. Leonie talked vaguely about walking into a door. She had no idea what the children were doing – anything. She was just waiting for the next time he'd push open the front door.

Then one day he didn't come. She went through the evening in a trance, and went to bed once the younger children were in. She left the door on the latch, and heard him when he swung it open. He grabbed her by the throat as she moved down the corridor towards him.

'Back to the bedroom, bitch!'

'No. Gary's there. We can't.'

'Get rid of him.'

She shook her head. 'Not tonight. Tomorrow.'

'Now.'

'I can't.'

He tightened his grip on her throat, then loosened it slowly. 'I'll have to make you wait for it then, till tomorrow, won't I?' He unclasped his hands, turned and left so quickly that she could not catch hold of his jacket, although she was running after him.

Gary cried when she told him he had to move beds. She was uncertain where to put him. If she put him in with Wayne and Darren they would torment him – and there was no question of putting him with the girls. If she put him in the sitting room he couldn't go to sleep till everyone else had gone to bed, and he needed to go to sleep early. In the end she decided to leave him in her room, making him a bed on the floor in the corner. He slept deeply – never stirred in the night – so why shouldn't he stay there? He wouldn't be any the wiser.

And for the first few nights it went smoothly. He whimpered when she put him to bed in his new place, and stretched out his arms to her bed, but she was firm, and by the time Bill arrived he was asleep.

Then Bill stayed all night. Leonie was woken in the morning by Gary's terrified howls. He had crept up to the bed to climb in with her, and come face to face with Bill.

'What's wrong with him?'

Leonie hugged the sobbing boy, his face buried in her shoulder.

'What's wrong with him, I said.'

'Nothing. He's – he's just a bit slow.'

'Mental, is he?'

'Yes.'

'Does he usually sleep with you?'

She nodded. Gary's sobs quietened.

'Do you fuck with him?'

Leonie turned to face Bill, who was propped up on one elbow in the bed, watching her. 'Get out.'

'He's a big lad.'

'Get out. Now.' Gary began to scream again, terrified by the tone of his mother's voice. Bill climbed out of bed and pulled his clothes on. When he was dressed he stood still, looking at Leonie.

'Get out, I said.'

He went.

He came back three days later, in the afternoon. And from then onwards he stayed at the flat two or three nights a week. Gary still cried at the sight of him, but he was learning to calm down more quickly. The boy became more withdrawn – his mother had hardly spoken to him for weeks, and although he painstakingly continued to make her cups of tea, she rarely acknowledged them or thanked him. Gary slept with his face to the wall, and no longer tried to creep into bed in the mornings – even when Bill wasn't there.

The other children were full of resentment. 'What have you brought him here for? We don't want him in our place!' There was no explanation Leonie could have articulated to herself, and she simply replied that it was hard luck, they'd have to put up with him. He and Wayne had a fight one night, on the way back from the pub – Wayne had been lying in wait for him. Bill must have thrashed him because Wayne didn't come home for a couple of days, and when he did it was only to collect his things. He told his mum he'd joined the army. Leonie said good, better than hanging about the estate with no job and no prospects. But when she heard he was going to Belfast she cried.

A year later Bill was living at the flat. Sex between himself and Leonie made up in violence what it had lost in intensity and frequency. The children all knew how violent he was, and were cautious not to cross his path. Donna was married now, and had a flat of her own. Lynda, who'd got a little baby, moved out after a couple of months, and stayed at Donna's. Leonie had told her she'd help out with the baby, but Lynda didn't dare to leave the child with her for fear of Bill. Tracey fixed a bolt to the inside of her bedroom door. Leonie, whose last dregs of will and self-determination seemed to have been drained by him, serviced him as she did the children – shopping, cleaning, washing, cooking. He gave her money from time to time, but she never knew when it would be, nor how much, and it was never enough.

Gary, more subdued and self-contained now, lived in total fear of him. Normally slow, fear had the effect of stunning him. If he was making a drink and Bill shouted, 'Hurry up with that!' he would spill it or continue to add more and more spoonfuls of sugar, or simply freeze in mid-air like a chameleon and be unable to continue at all until Bill's attention shifted from him. His misery was compounded by the fact that, when startled, he sometimes wet himself.

Leonie defended him. It was the only thing that ever made her turn on Bill. The other children knew she would do nothing if he knocked them about – they knew he hit her, anyway. But when he started on Gary, she was ready to fight.

'Leave him alone, you bullying bastard. You lay a finger on him and I'll kill you.' Bill usually backed down. But if ever he was on his own in the room with Gary, he would start to taunt him. 'Thick head. Throwback. Loony.' And pull faces, with lolling tongue and rolling eyes. The boy lived in terror.

Bill's comings and goings were erratic. He was generally out during the daytime, and sometimes for the evening and night as well. There was a constant tension in the air because of the fear of his return, since no one knew when that would be; but when he hadn't appeared by 6.30, Leonie and Gary, and Darren and Tracey if they were in, would eat their tea together then sit around the telly in fragile peace. Leonie would put her arm around the boy's shoulders and he would rest his head against her.

Once when Bill came in he marched straight up behind them, where they were sitting on the sofa, and struck Gary's head sharply with the side of his hand.

'Grow up, you fucking baby.' Gary began to cry and Leonie started shouting at Bill. He slammed her in the face too, and went out to the kitchen, where he broke every plate and dish, hurling them against the wall.

Tracey comforted her mother, when she was sure Bill had gone out. 'Why d'you have him here? We don't have to put up with this. Just lock the door and don't let him back.'

But Leonie, bleeding from the nose, her arms around a sobbing Gary, shook her head. He was hurting her children, beating her up, destroying her life. The physical need he had served for her was long gone. But she knew it was impossible for him not to come back. Like an animal on its journey to the slaughterhouse, Leonie knew she hadn't arrived there yet. She had never made a conscious choice in her life; you get herded and pushed where they want you to go. And there are a few times when your own dumb animal instinct – for food, sex, survival – drags you down a one-way route. Had there been any choice? At the point at which she leant in the kitchen doorway, watching him paint, unable to support herself for the weight of desire in her limbs? No.

She accepted her own powerlessness in the face of the evil that had entered their lives.

Since cruelty to Gary was the only thing that provoked a reaction from Leonie (even the dumb animal protects her defenceless young), Bill began to persecute the boy more systematically. He shouted at him suddenly for no reason, and laughed at the boy's panic and distress. If he could creep up behind Gary he would slap his head or pull his hair.

One night when Leonie lay still as a lump of lard beneath him, he suggested waking Gary up. It produced the desired effect; she began to scratch and wrestle with him, and he had to fight to hold her down. They rolled off the bed and on to the floor, and Bill, who had achieved his aim as they made contact with the floor, climbed off her and back into bed. He fell asleep immediately, and only noticed that Leonie was still on the floor when he woke an hour later. She felt cold. He heaved her up on to the bed. She was breathing, so he slapped her face a couple of times but there was no response. After a while he slipped out of bed, dressed, and left.

When Leonie came round she could not remember what had happened. She had a bad headache, and felt sick.

Mon. 24

What's the matter with you, Marion? You're making me sick. Rubbing my nose in dirt, like a dog. Leave it, for Christ's sake.

Perhaps she likes to write it. Does it give her a thrill? Perhaps she likes the power: watching characters caged like rats. Perhaps she likes to line them up along the edge of the pale, and slowly, one by one, push them beyond. She likes dirt. If you give her the *News of the Screws* she'll read it before she throws it away. Isn't it disgusting? Ooh, let's look a bit closer. Just hand on while I fetch my camera – God, I can hardly bear to look. Ooh!

Is that her? Perhaps it turns her on. That careful cataloguing of pornographic detail, of lust, of violence – the slow burning moves of Leonie from the

bedroom to Bill, the tension and climax on the page –
doesn't she love it? Perhaps she's Leonie and wants
to be beaten; she's a woman, all she needs is a good
thumping and a fuck. How do I know what she's up
to, under that long black narrator's mantle – and then
under that reader's cloak of respectability: what are
you up to? Enjoying yourself, are you? Getting hot?
Marion?

Leave.

Leave and away. It's enough. Listen.

What am I doing with Leonie? Why dabble in this?
I can walk about my quiet, pleasing room, where I
have spent the time since I've been ill. The room is
simple: white walls, blue woodwork, deep blue
carpet. Blue curtains with white spots; and a faded
candlewick bedspread that doesn't match, and eases
me. From the window the view is small: an enclosed,
snow-filled garden, bordered by a garage and a
hedge of snow-covered domestic firs, green-black
and white. I like this room, I am living in this room.
The luxury in this room is the table and chair, an
unpretentious white formica table, at which I sit, in
comfort, by the window – and write Leonie. Now
why?

Maybe it's letting something out. Like lancing a
boil; letting the pus and poison which have made a
hurting pressure flow out on to the page through my
moving pen. Even though it never happened to me.
In one form or another, dirt will out.

Maybe. Before, while I was writing, I thought, this
is the worst. I am drawing the bottom line, the base
level, people sunk to half-formed animals in the
slime and now I'll know it can't be any worse.
Wanting to know the worst, as a child strains its eyes
in the darkness to make out the evil face of the beast
that haunts its dreams. Yes, I want to know the

worst. But once I've looked up from the page and broken the hold of that 'worst', it's milk and water. There are always worse. Tortures, gas chambers, massacres, people who take little children and –

There's no bottom to evil, if I dive in for a penny at the deep end, I'll be sinking still for ever. It goes on down.

All right then. These combine. There is a thing to be let out. It is to be named. Naming it will let it out, and I will know it. I imagine it a creature in a sack, something alive and vicious with fear, like a ferret or a pig or a wild cat, tied in a sack. The story is the sack; inside it is the thing I know, the creature I know well. I can't name the creature, it is too familiar to describe. But I can make a sack for it, and in the sack the beast threshes about – tenses, scrabbles in frenzy, feigns sleep. The sack moves, stretches, sags: it can resemble different things. But inside it the creature remains the same. The sack is the clearest I can get to naming it, containing it – dumping it outside the door for someone else to take away.

It won't go away, of course. It's my beast, it lives with me. But each time I bag it, catch it in a sack – no matter how ugly and unfamiliar the shape it makes – at each capture I strike a blow for freedom, diminish its power to harm. I will know it.

———————

Bill did not return for eight days. As each day passed, it became more possible to consider the thought that he might not return at all. The days were long; fragile, suspended time waiting for a thunderstorm to break, a bomb to fall. Time long in its isolated acts of tenderness, Leonie's arm around Gary's shoulder as they sit watching telly; Gary's jump of fear when the door is opened; the mutual wryness of relief as it's Tracey who comes in, not Bill. Leonie daren't let Gary back into her bed, although she longs for his warm comfort; but when he goes to bed she sits with him, legs tucked under the sheets, to read him a bedtime comic as she used to, long ago, before Bill came. In the silence and space she can see Gary again; his beautiful spreading smile, his timidity, his desire to please. He's such a good boy to her, for no reason, her eyes keep filling with tears.

On the eighth day there was a knock at the door. She didn't guess it was Bill, because he'd always walked straight in. When she opened it he stared at her, then pushed her aside and walked in in silence. Gary was sitting at the table, laboriously filling a sheet of paper with uneven letters. She'd been finding him things to do because he was lost, in the holidays – he always was – moping around without his school to go to. What she'd do when he finished there she didn't know. Bill ripped the sheet from under the boy's pen in a single movement, and Gary froze, a look of terror on his face. Bill glanced at the uneven jumble of letters on the page then crumpled it and hurled it viciously into a corner.

'What you got him doing?' he shouted. 'Think he can write? That thick cretin?' With a snort of contempt he cuffed Gary across the head then barged out of the room to slump in front of the telly. 'Cup of tea!' he shouted. Leonie put her arms around Gary's head, cradling it to her breast. The boy was crying quietly, and they both froze into silence as the man's threatening voice rose a pitch.

'Cup of tea, I said, you fucking idle cow. Now!' Leonie moved automatically to put the kettle on, and Gary sat at the table, his arms by his sides, staring ahead of him. He had wet himself, and the urine dripped slowly from the chair to the floor below. As she made the tea she watched the way he sat unmoving, hopeless, like a dog.

She gave Bill his tea in silence and he turned on her, raising his voice above the telly.

'Haven't you got a civil word for me, bitch? Lost your tongue? I bet you were gabbing to that retard before I came in, weren't you? What's wrong with me?'

She shook her head in silence, turning away, but he grabbed her arm and twisted it up behind her back. Involuntarily, she screamed. Gary's white face appeared in the doorway.

'Let me go, you bastard.' Gary, standing in the doorway, began to clap his hands with terror, shouting, 'No no no no' in rhythm, like a football supporter.

'Doncha like it?' Bill leered at him. He yanked Leonie's arm up a notch.

'No no no no no!' The boy's high-pitched voice was nearly screaming.

'Wanta see what grownups do, Gary?' asked Bill. 'Wanta see what big men do to women?' Bending Leonie's arm he forced her to the ground, and holding her twisted arm still with his right he yanked up her skirt with his left, and began to tear at her underclothes. 'It's what your Mummy likes to do, kid. Has she done it with you, eh? Better ask her to, eh?'

'Nuh nuh nuh nuh nuh –' The boy's voice was a whisper now, his face round-eyed and terrified, his hands bumping together in a fast frenzy. Bill fumbled at his zip, finally letting go Leonie's arm to get two hands to it, and she managed to rear up and hit him. They fought across the room, knocking over the sofa, and Leonie screamed 'Help me, Gary!'

The boy stood rooted to the spot, shaking his head now to the same intolerable rhythm as his hands, the heels only meeting in a swift pattering drumbeat accompaniment. Bill was stronger, and pinioned her again on the other side of the overturned sofa. He made a few quick thrusts, grunted, and was off within a minute. As Leonie heaved herself up, gasping for breath, she looked at the boy's face and saw that he was not even seeing her; his eyes, fixed on the middle distance, were lost in a trance of terror. Bill pushed past him in the doorway, thumping him on the shoulder as he went.

'That's what big boys do, Gary. They stick it in, see.' She heard him go into the bedroom and slam the door. Her arm ached badly where he'd twisted it. She pulled her clothes around her and crossed to Gary.

'Nuh nuh nuh nuh – ' The trembling head and twitching hands continued their motion, the breaths quick with terror.

'Gary,' she said. 'Gary, you thick bastard – shut it.' She shook him roughly by the shoulders. 'Quiet.'

She led him into the kitchen and made him sit down. There was silence.

'Cup of tea,' she said. 'Shall we make a cup of tea?'

He did not reply. Leonie sat down carefully at the other end of the table, and began to cry.

He's my baby. He's mine. I made him. And when he come back – after that meningitis – all sad and floppy – it's me what coped with it. Me what stayed up nights, nursing him. Me what changed his nappies and mopped up his piss and shit for years, not months like with the others. Me what loved him.

He's mine. Right. He's like – part of me. Still. With not growing up like the others. Part of me close up, like he never went away. He's – you know the smell of shit? Someone else's shit smells horrible, don't it? Someone else's shit stinks. Not your baby's, though. My babies' shit never stank to me. It's all right, you don't mind it. You can scrape it off their bums or find it plastered all over the cot and you get on and clean it up. You don't mind. But when they get bigger – If I go on the bog after Darren now the stink of him makes me heave. It does.

Not Gary. He's bigger but his shit's still like my own, to me. I can breathe it in, it's warm in my nose like my own.

He's mine. I've got him. What's he got? He's got me. He hasn't got nothing else, for Christ's sake. What's he got? Who else ever give a toss for him? He's got – he's got those teachers, that school. But when he's finished there they'll say so what and get on with the new kids. He's done for.

Who loves him? Me. I made him and his little world, his clever things and his safe places, his little treats. I know what's good for him. I know what he likes. I know he's got to live – he's got to live.

He's mine. There's only me. He's got nothing else. There's nothing else for him, only me, I've got to keep him safe.

I done it, right? For years, I done it. Kept them off – everyone laughing, calling him, teasing him, the other kids mucking him about. I kept him safe. I'm his Mum. I keep him safe from people – tormenting him. From hurt. From fear.

So when – when –

That's what I do. I keep him safe.

The following evening she was putting away the clean clothes in her bedroom, and Gary was washing up for her, when she heard the front door slam. Bill was back again. She heard him shout something at Gary. She opened her bedroom door and stood at the crack. The sound of the TV started suddenly, and she could hear the creak of Bill throwing himself into an armchair.

'Where's your Mum, thicko?' she heard him shout. Gary did not reply. 'Wanta see her get her knickers off again? D'ya like that, dumbo?'

No reply. She heard Bill curse half-heartedly, as if exasperated, then change channels. The volume of the TV increased. She opened the door wider. She could see along the corridor, through the open kitchen door at the end Gary's back – at the sink, washing up. He was standing completely still, his shoulders hunched, hands in the bowl. After she'd been watching a few minutes, and the voices on the telly had run on uninterrupted, he moved, and began carefully rubbing at a plate. Very slowly, and completely silently, like a woman in a trance, Leonie began to move along the corridor towards him. When she got to the threshold of the kitchen she didn't pause, but her right hand stretched out, skimming the top of the table, catching up the bread knife. Her movements were those of a sleep-walker; around her the room seemed turned to slow motion, each movement, each action flowing slowly across minutes. Gary picked up a mug, swished it through the water, raised it slowly to his face and peered into it. Slowly, he turned it upside-down and watched the last drips fall from it; carefully he placed it in the rack. She was behind him. Some sixth sense made him half-turn his head, eyes staring with fear, and he came face to face with her. His terrified expression relaxed slowly into a full smile, and after they had smiled at one another in silence he gave a little nod and turned back to his dishes. She raised her left hand to his shoulder, slid the forearm round and across his neck, in a hug. He snuggled his chin against her arm, raising another mug for careful inspection as he did so. Leonie lifted the knife at arm's length from her body, like a cellist about to play, and drew it across and in over his throat.

As blade touched flesh, slow motion stopped. Gary bucked and tried to jerk backwards, and Leonie, supporting his skinny weight against her body, began to saw at his neck like a woman cutting fresh bread with a blunt knife. The small sharp teeth moved through the resistant cartilage, sticking twice but moved on by Leonie's pumping elbow. On the right side before the left, blood began to ooze, then to spurt, from the boy's neck into the washing-up bowl, on to Leonie's arms, into her face.

Sorry? I should be glad. He's safe now. Warm, dark, all folded in – just like he was a little baby in my belly, before all this started. He was safe then, and perfect – and he is now. I never hurt him. I saved him. I ask you – what sort of a mother could hurt her own little child?

As Gary fell she crumpled with him, falling heavily, half on top of him. She pulled the knife out and slid it across the kitchen floor, away from her. Bill, who had been watching from the doorway since an odd sound interrupted his viewing, stepped quickly back. But Leonie did not see him. She crawled off Gary's back, and round to his head. Kneeling before him, she raised his head on to her lap, and rhythmically smoothed his hair away from his face. Blood continued to flow from the wound on to her skirt and, soaking through it, to her thighs, but she did not seem to notice.

I've been here nearly two weeks now. I'm better, it's time to go. There has been no fresh snow for a few days, and during the daytime the sun shines. Gradually the thick white encrustations are reduced, the disappearance of snow seems a possibility. But every night it freezes hard, and the snow which was turning to water in daylight is preserved as glassy ice. In next day's sunlight that ice begins to thaw, then at night it refreezes. The shapes of snow-covered objects change each day.

Wed. 26

I drove thirty miles or so yesterday, which was enough. I was exhausted when I arrived. I wonder now at that relentless energy which kept me going in the first week, how could I keep on driving. I am in a small village on a main road, surrounded by wide exposed fields. The minor roads are either blocked or threaten to become so. My room is in one of the village's two pubs. They don't get many tourists this time of year. This morning I went out and walked along the lane that crosses the main road. The sun was shining and I could almost feel its warmth on my face. Underfoot the black ice was covered in a thin slushy layer. The snow is dirty, by the edges of the road it's filthy, and even in the fields it's grey and grained. My shoes are not waterproof, or else I might have walked farther, enjoying the immediacy of sunshine, snow, sharp cold air.

The fairy story I remember best is of red dancing shoes. A little girl wanted red shoes very badly, and finally she got some. They were magical, they danced and danced. At last the girl was tired and cried to the shoes, 'Enough, please stop, please – dance no more!'

But the shoes would not be still, they made her dance along lanes, across fields, through woods and ditches, up hills and over dales till her feet bled and she was dropping from exhaustion – and still they danced. In the end they danced her to the executioner's cottage, and she begged him to chop off her dancing feet with his great axe. The hideous stumps of feet danced off in the wicked red shoes, and the little girl got crutches. That wasn't enough, though; the shoes and feet still danced about in her way to plague her – her only escape was death. Her death was full of bliss, I remember, her heart burst with joy; that wicked girl who dared to want.

My grandmother kept such books in the room where I slept when I stayed with her. They were in a tall glass-fronted cabinet. I could never think of it as a bookcase, it was the sort of furniture I expected to see china displayed in. The books were tall, bound in brown leather, with three ridges reminding me of knuckles, in their spines. They had marbled endpapers, which looked like the patterns oil makes in water. On the bottom shelf, *Encyclopaedia*, twelve volumes. On the top shelf, *Birds of the World*. On the middle shelf, Maps and Cautionary Tales. I read them secretly. I wasn't allowed to open the cabinet. The books were old and valuable. The tales convinced me that every act has its price. The boy who told a lie was run over by a hackney carriage. The girl who spied through a keyhole was merely blinded. The greedy child was brought low with a lingering disease akin to starvation. The only safe course of action was to do nothing. The less you did, the safer you were.

The Twins

Write down about the twins.

What must I say?

Write the truth. Last May I gave birth to healthy unidentical twins; Penny 5lb 2oz, Paul 5lb exactly.

I have been sitting staring at the wall, with my pen held above the paper, till my arm aches. What must I write?

Tell about the twins.

I have twin babies, who were born to me in the normal way, and came home with me from hospital after a week. They are my children.

Go on.

After they were born my life changed. I was unhappy. They cried a lot. I could not sleep. Gareth wasn't there. Then Ruth and Vi.

Now as I try to write those old hopeless tears are coursing down my face and I still don't know why or who for. How can I find the source of my grief, how can it ever be repaired?

How can I talk of them? I don't know what words to use, what names to give things. The facts are simple but explain nothing to me.

List the facts.

I did not love them.

I was a bad mother.

I did not know how to look after them. They cried, they did not sleep. I could not make a routine. I couldn't tell day from night.

They were angry and colicky and I could not comfort them.

They did not like me.

These are the facts. I lived like a pig. I couldn't do things. I didn't take them out in the fresh air, I didn't play with them, I didn't wash their hair. I was no good.

The facts are not the texture of that time. The texture is

insubstantial, lacking all facts. The texture is that I know nothing. I am in bed, one of them is feeding, the boy has the right, the girl the left, the girl is greedier, the left is bigger. I know nothing. I cry. Time is grey and trailing, there are thin dusty grey veils of net curtain trailing all around my head so that whatever I look at it is in the way. Nothing is clear, nothing is real. These babies are not what I thought I would have. I was going to have Ruth again, Vi again. These babies hate me, they know I am no good. When they fall asleep I creep out of the room, my stomach is in a knot for fear of the slightest noise which might disturb them. I creep to the kitchen. I want to make some tea for the girls. I am shaking with hunger, I scoff some yoghurt and a pint of milk, I have to sit down. My body is heavy, every move I make is against a pull of gravity one hundred times stronger than it used to be. The weight of each hair on my head is terrible. I don't know what is in the fridge, the cupboard. Other people have put food there. People come into my house, I don't know who. I try to find something to cook quickly. I start to open a tin of tomatoes. My fingers are like water, they don't have the strength to turn the key on the opener. Listen.

One is crying. I must get it before it wakes the other. As I pick it up I am weeping in hopeless rage. Why won't it sleep? I take it in the kitchen to feed, boy on the right. The tomatoes are open, onion chopped, but the pepper hasn't been sliced. I can't move, I watch the clock ticking, the boy feeds. The washing must go on, the drier, the cooking, I must feed the other one, I must change them, my back is breaking my body is heavy. I've done it wrong. I stink, I must have a bath, I must bath them, I must change the sheets, I must play with them, I must go to the toilet, I must be dressed when the girls come home from school.

I can do nothing. The tasks pile up in mountains around me. At my first move to shift one pebble of one mountain that blocks my way, a baby starts to cry. They have stopped me in my life, in time, like a cartoon character who's had a bucket of sticky toffee poured over her. I try to move and the glutinous sticky stuff pulls my hand or foot back again. I am stuck like a fly on paper.

I started to go away before. Once I put all my clothes on, in the bathroom, shaking and sweating. I was sweating terribly. I crept to the front door. As my hand touched the latch one started to cry. I wanted to open the door. I was trying to open the door and go out while they were sleeping. The other woke up, they both began to scream. What must I do? Is this my life? I sit on the floor by the door, I cannot stop crying.

Go back, get them up, they are both screaming. I can't feed them together, I can't do it right. The health visitor with her little book and diagrams of feeding positions.

'You'll be feeding all night,' says she, 'unless you learn to feed them simultaneously.' They are too big, their heads are too heavy. I can't do it. They must feed one at a time, it's all I can do. They might as well feed all night. I don't sleep. Now they are both awake, that's the worst thing. While the girl feeds the boy screams. I go into the lounge with her and shut the door but I can still hear him, it makes me frantic. His breast starts to leak.

I don't know what happened. All the days and nights ran into a blur, I did not know what was happening, the girls came and went and I tried to keep a grip but my fingers slipped all the time I kept falling. They helped, they brought more people to help. They shopped, they cooked, there was a cleaning lady. Then a doctor – one, two, I don't know. I knew what to do, I've done it. I know how to look after babies.

He told me to eat and sleep. At night I lay waiting for the next one to wake up, crying in rage because I wasn't asleep. It was no good, I didn't know how to do it. I pretended I did but I didn't. Did I ever look after Ruth and

Vi? Was it me? I made it up, none of it happened like that, there were no days of measured contentment. I'm a liar. I write lies.

I see the doctor's big fat face, he's standing over the bed with his coat on, rushing off to an emergency, wasting time with me. He says I'm silly, I'm ill. Take the tablets. Start to take care of yourself. You must take the tablets, you must wean these babies, you haven't the energy to feed them. Have you heard of post-natal depression? The tablets will go through into your milk. You must wean them or you could make your babies ill. Take the tablets, wean the babies, get some sleep. You'll be better in a month if you do as I say.

Vi is there. She says don't cry. She says it will get better, honestly Mum. You must do what he says now. Please. You'll get better. It'll be all right, see?

At night which is so terribly long while I sit in the dark with the boy on the right or the girl on the left, listening to the house creaking around me, and cars in the night streets outside, I stop crying. I must stop feeding them. I am no good to them. Their crying drives me mad, I only want them to sleep. I don't want to hurt them, but I want them to sleep. I want them to leave me alone.

Do what the man says, then. Take the tablets, sleep, let them leave you alone. Let them cry at the bottle, instead of you.

Then what? This baby is sucking at my breast. While it sucks, it is quiet. I give it food. I am their food. Nothing else. No good to Ruth or Vi. No good to them, even, but as food. I am their food.

And if I can't even give them that – if I can't even feed them – I am no good at all.

All right. I know what to do. But while they want it, at least I can provide milk. If I can't do anything else for them, at least I can do that.

I fed them. I was a milk machine. He said, 'Loss of

appetite is a symptom', but I was not ill. I can choose to be bad, not mad. I was ravenous. I ate dry sliced bread from the packet, I ate chocolate biscuits, I made the girls bring me cheese and apples and ryebread. I ate tuna fish out of the tin with my fingers, I drank yoghurt from the pot while they fed. Making milk, like a giant cow gone mad and trying to stuff the world down its gullet to make it into milk.

If I can't do anything else, I can do that. At least, I can feed them.

9 p.m.

I went for a walk. There was a bitter wind, the sky is leaden, it will snow again tonight. Everything is at zero point, locked into this eternal winter. Beneath the snow and ice you sense the final death of plants, the last resistance they held in reserve for the spring has been clinched out of them by the cold. Only freezing holds the world up; if the ice ever melts it will all fall down and lie, sodden and limp, on the ground. I am full of ice.

There is no point in writing this. What is there to be found, in the dregs of the last eight months? I had the twins. I made a mistake. Which was simply the latest in a long line stretching back to Ruth's birth, maybe before. The right thing for the wrong reason. The wrong thing for the right reason. What does it matter, finally? It's ordinary.

I'll tell another story. Other people's stories are better. They have shape. I'm sick of this endless going on from day to day. I'll write a life whose shape is tight and firm, drawn on the page like a pattern. A woman who stole a baby. Her story; her reasons, the subterranean links under years, between one thought, one chance event, and a growth in the imagination which will materilize half a lifetime later. The story is circular, satisfying . . .

You're playing, Marion. Hiding, bluffing. I don't know what you're up to. Your list isn't finished.

Thurs. 27

It's morning; the sun has just come up into a clear blue sky, and is catching the snow with pink splashes of light. Everything is frozen still, and unreally beautiful in the late dawn light. What was pointless and hopeless last night is maybe still so, but I said I would tidy up, and the list isn't done. Jackie's not on the list yet.

* * *

Jackie. When she came back she said, 'You're in a mess, Marion. Why didn't you write? Why didn't you let me know?'

I said, 'I'm all right Jackie, leave me alone.'

'No.'

'I'm busy. I've got to put the washing on.'

'I'm taking you out. Helen can babysit.'

'I don't want to come out. I'm all right. Go away.'

Jackie was my friend. Jackie was in the ward sixteen years ago when they brought me up after having Ruth. Her Helen was one day old. Like two excited dogs we yapped and nipped and chased each other across that first year of their lives, from crisis to crisis, from exhilarated discovery to latest breakthrough, from commiserations to confessions. When she went back to work I was sorry for her. But she was sorry for me that I didn't. After a while we were both sorry for ourselves as well, when we realized neither of us could have everything.

I was really, complacently sorry for her when I was huge

with the twins and she came round to tell me about Hong Kong.

'It's only six months,' she kept saying. 'It's a fantastic opportunity. And Helen's coming out for a holiday when she's finished her O levels.'

I tried to imagine working in Hong Kong for six months, and being parted from the girls for however long it was before they came to join me 'for a holiday'. I was glad I couldn't imagine it. I promised to ask Helen round a lot, and write. I did neither.

My friend Jackie. Nights in the kitchen, late, when we've been sitting talking and talking ourselves out, unravelling all the events and thoughts and half-thoughts and theories, holding our lives up to each other for verification, making each other real. It was too late by January. She brought back Christmas presents for the twins, little Chinese silken suits, emerald green and peacock blue. 'The blue's for the girl,' she told me. She was expansive and happy, she'd been promoted, she said I ought to see a doctor.

So I told her I had, and I had tablets, thank you, and I didn't want her fucking help any more than I wanted anyone else's.

* * *

Karate nights. Why do I remember them? Ruth started karate when she was thirteen, so Vi must have been eleven. We used to go and meet her, at nine when it finished. In the autumn we walked, I was glad to be outside after the artificial light and heat of the library. Vi was full of the comp., all those new people; she rattled on to me about teachers and school and I half-listened while I scuffed my feet amongst the fallen leaves and remembered new autumn terms myself, new shoes, frosty mornings, conkers. Vi would talk about anything, she never stopped.

I think she liked to have me to herself.

Those evenings were a chore in theory, having to go out at eight-thirty broke up the evening to nothing. When the nights got darker and wetter we'd go in the car and quite often stop at the Italian café for a cappuccino and apricot tart, or a water ice. It became a ritual, he smiled at us in recognition when we arrived. Ruth was nearly always in a good mood, flushed with exercise and self-confidence, explaining movements to Vi. The coffee was frothy, with grated chocolate on top; Vi scooped if off delicately with a spoon, and licked it like a lollipop. I don't know what we talked about – but we were always talking, always buzzing. They stand out clear, the karate evenings.

* * *

Vi. Vi is soft-hearted. Vi comes into my room when she gets back from school, she looks at the twins and seems to like them. I watch her pick one up and sit on the bed, holding it, touching its small claw-fingers with her free hand, smiling patiently until the slow-focusing eyes can capture her. Then the baby smiles at Vi and Vi laughs at the baby. I get off the bed irritably, gather up mugs. Without looking up she says mildly,

'I've put the kettle on, Mum.' I go into the kitchen to watch it.

She has a little girl's face still; little girl's shoulder-length straight hair, which she sometimes plaits; little girl's wide-open eyes and slightly upturned nose. She's taller than Ruth already, lean and rounded and growing. I used to look at her and think, like I did when she was a toddler, 'What a lovely body.' And I thought – not that I created it single-handed – but that its perfection was through me, of me. The beauty and firmness of her limbs – a share of it – was mine to delight in.

Vi pushes me. If I look up from the bed or the baby I'm

holding I notice she's come in, she's walking round my room picking up tissues and cotton wool and dropping them into a plastic bag, then she takes out the nappies. She comes back with a tray and loads up the cups and yoghurt pots and banana peels. I don't meet her eye. Then she says,

'Do you need any shopping?' I don't reply.

'Mum? It's a nice day. Shall we put them in the pram and take them out?'

'They're quiet now, Vi. If they wake up.' When they woke up I fed them and changed them and by then it was one and a half hours later and Vi had gone out.

'Mum? Don't get mad – can I make a suggestion? Look, I was talking to Dad and he's really upset – he is, honestly – and he asked me what he could do so I suggested –'

'What?'

'Well, why don't we get a cleaning lady for a bit and he could pay her, and then you wouldn't have to worry about that and you could just concentrate on the twins and getting better and –'

I was just looking at her. I watched her falter into silence, and then pick up again in anger.

'Look, I know you think me and Ruth should do it all but it's not working, Mum. We've been doing it for weeks. We're at school, we've got work to do, you can't expect us to run the house, get the food, cook and clear up and everything – it just doesn't work. It puts everyone under pressure – you make us feel guilty as soon as we come in the door – it's horrible coming into this house, and you act as if it's our fault they're here and you're ill, as if we've got to pay you back or something –' She burst into tears. I didn't say anything. I didn't care what they did. Let him pay for a cleaner if they want one.

When the cleaner came I shut my bedroom door. She knocked on it but I didn't answer. But I couldn't sleep because of the roar of the vacuum cleaner, and the idiotic babble of daytime TV that she kept on while she worked. When it went quiet I crept out to the kitchen to find a drink and she was sitting at the kitchen table as if she owned it, reading a magazine and eating sandwiches. I went back to bed and she brought me lunch on a tray, then she looked at them and said how sweet they were. I wanted to leave it but I was starving.

* * *

Ruth. Ruth didn't come and sit on the bed. I didn't know if she was in or out. Sometimes Vi said, 'Ruth's gone to Gareth's', or 'Ruth's gone to Annie's', sometimes not. Sometimes when I asked where she was tonight Vi said, 'Up in her room', in amazement, as if I must be mad.

She came to the bedroom door sometimes to offer a cup of tea or food. She never even looked at the twins, it was as if she was pretending they didn't exist. I wanted to shake her. But I couldn't even have grabbed hold of her. She never came quite that near. She kept away from me, she was disappearing, her face was hidden. I wanted to catch her, or shout, 'Come here!' but I was afraid of what they would think. Or of breaking something, by shouting that – breaking something tenuous and fragile, so that she would slip out of sight behind the doorpost, out of the other room, out of the house, like a helium balloon when the string breaks.

* * *

The day Vi came to tell me. I hadn't noticed, but Ruth had already gone. It's like a faulty television, the pictures are all reduced to varying shades of grey, with lines of marching dots across them, and a faint angry crackle overlying the sound. The pictures stop and start again in a different place.

It's like slow motion. Everything goes slow. I sit on the bed and remember what I'm looking for. Clean bra. I look around the floor. I must get rid of those nappies. I think I can see a bra under the blue cot. But it's dirty. The boy wakes up, I put him over my shoulder. I sit down again. I've forgotten what I'm looking for. He needs changing. What did I do with the cotton wool? Vi comes in. She stands looking at me for a bit.

'Aren't you at school?'

'It's Saturday. Shall I open the window?' I can see the cotton wool on the windowsill so I go and fetch it. It's raining outside.

'No. It's cold.'

'Are you putting him to bed, Mum?'

'I'm changing him.'

'Shall I?'

'No. It's all right.' She sits on the bed and watches me, I can't find the Vaseline. She is watching my every move. 'Why don't you make us a cup of tea?'

'OK,' she says. 'D'you want to come and have it in the kitchen? I bought a cake.' She goes out, which is a relief. I sit down again. When I hear the kettle whistling I remember she's making tea so I change the boy on the bed. The sheet's dirty anyway. The changing mat must be in the bathroom. I put him back and put his thumb in his mouth. He won't sleep.

She is cutting me a slice of chocolate cake, the tea is steaming. I start to eat the cake quickly, it sharpens me up. I sit down and look at her. What's going on?

'Ruth and me have been talking, Mum.' She pours tea. 'We think it's very hard work for you, with the twins, even though you're a lot better now.'

'Oh.'

'We've been thinking it might be better – it might make it a bit easier on you – if we went and stayed with Dad for a bit.'

'With Gareth? In the flat?'

'Well, no – you see, what he's doing – well actually, he's buying a house. He's buying a house in Stoke Newington – we've been to see it. It's pretty tatty but it'll be great when it's done up, and he said he'd like us to help decorate anyway.'

'A big house? He's bought a big house?'

'I think he's buying it with Linda. I think she's buying half.' Vi gets up and boils more water and fusses with the teapot. I finish my cake. It is quiet.

'Mum – I'm not . . .' She doesn't finish.

'You and Ruth want to live there?'

'Not live – just, you know, for a bit. Look, it makes a lot of sense; you've got your hands full and hardly get any sleep and aren't well anyway, so it's no good for you having to worry about where we are at teatime and what's going on. And he nearly always ends up giving us lifts home which is a bit rough on him because he's got to bring us back here then go all the way back there, I mean, it's a waste of petrol really. And it's not – well, more peace and quiet would probably be better for you, and I think – in the long run –'

Silence.

'It will be better in the long run, Mum, because it's quite hard for me and especially for Ruth with her exams, living here because it's so tense and you feel – well, we feel, it makes us feel guilty but there's nothing we can do. So that'll probably be a relief to you too, won't it? If we're not here feeling like that. It means we'll come and see you because we want to, instead of having to. And we won't be a responsibility to you. He can worry about how late we stay up, and all that.' Vi pretends to laugh.

One of them starts to cry. I go automatically to pick it up. She follows me.

'It will work out better in lots of ways, for now. Dad was saying it might be nice for you if Aunt Sarah came and stayed for a bit, it might make a break – she could have my room. And we get on with Linda OK, I mean she won't interfere with us – it'll be good for us really, like we're learning gradually to get more independent.'

I sit on the bed and give the baby my tit. Vi is standing in the doorway looking at me. 'Yes, yes,' I say. 'That'll be fine. Of course.'

She stands and looks at me a bit longer, as if she thinks I'll say something else. Then she goes away.

* * *

After they'd gone. The house is quiet, I'm on my own. Except for the twins.

I leave the landing light on – in case of burglars? Or for the girls? I wait for them to come home.

I know they're not coming, but part of my head still carries on, with 'They're late, they'll be tired for school. What can they be doing at this time of night?' I nearly phone Gareth to see if he's picking them up from somewhere, before I remember that they're not to be my concern.

When I go to bed I lie listening for them. But they don't live here any more. I think I'll ring Gareth anyway just to be told they're safe in bed, then I'll be able to sleep. If I know, definitely, that they are safely tucked up in bed. It's the not knowing, not even knowing if worrying is necessary.

I open the curtains. My room is darker than outside. Cars go by, lights shine in other houses. Are Ruth and Vi together? Are they in a car that might crash? Or walking along a street where a man is waiting, lurking in the shadows between two houses? Where are they? And if they don't go home, will he tell me? When? Will he wait till morning? Or might he ring me to see if they've come here?

117

They won't come here. They've taken their duvets to Gareth's. They are at Gareth and Linda's, talking, drinking cocoa, laughing, watching a late-night film, finishing painting their new bedroom door. They are in a different life.

When I go back to bed I can't sleep because my feet are freezing. The twins should wake soon. They are both snuffling, their noses blocked. I get up and put on my socks.

* * *

Vi was wrong about me and Gareth. We didn't pretend to be a devoted couple. It was her imagination that demanded that.

Like mine.

If a child can't have what it wants it has a screaming tantrum. It doesn't want something else, an alternative. It throws it on the floor, and screams. It would rather smash everything.

We did live together; you can't pretend to live in the same house. We did. He was always there at night, his possessions were there, his clothes were there. We were both parents to Ruth and Vi. We talked about them, worried about them, made plans concerning them. We both took them into account. We both paid for them.

We were husband and wife. Distantly, cynically, warily. In separate beds, and with a chilling respect for one another's privacy. But we knew each other better than anyone else. So well that there were no rules. Ruth and Vi thought it disgusting that I got pregnant. I know they did. (Disgusting of me, of course, not of Gareth. Double standards in my liberated daughters. Ruth may even despise me for it – see it as a deliberate attempt to blackmail him?) They are both wrong.

August. They were both away in France for a week with

118

school, and it was hot. Gareth and I didn't discuss it, but I assumed he would stay at Linda's most of the time, since the girls weren't at home. I was going to have an idle week, weeding the garden and reading some real adult novels, instead of all that teenage crap from work. I remember I bought a pile of Viragos and King Penguins, and settled in the sun on the lawn. Gareth came out into the garden on the first afternoon. I was surprised.

'Aren't you at work?'

'I came to fetch a script I need for a meeting tonight. You look like you're on holiday. This weather – can I join you?'

I said yes, and he went to put his shorts on. He came out with a bottle of white wine and some ice. We lay in the sun and drank and talked – I don't know, about books, the girls, work – for an hour or more. It was easy, completely easy. We knew each other so well. He leant over and stroked my leg, and we looked at each other. Yes.

We were in a hurry, we didn't get further than the lounge – the French windows were still open and I said, 'What if someone comes round the back?' and he said, 'We'll charge them fifty pounds for the performance' and his skin was hot and dry and the smell of him made me tremble.

Before he left he said, 'Can I come back tonight?' The house was empty, the girls were away. We didn't have to be together. We made love in every room in the house, that week, as if we were marking out a territory. Nothing else existed. When Linda rang I reached for the phone by the side of the bed and told her I didn't know where he was. He was inside me. It wasn't revenge, I knew he wasn't giving her up. It wasn't anything except what it was. Knowing each other as we did. As we do.

After the girls came back it stopped. It was the last time, because soon after I found I was pregnant, and then he was angry.

* * *

With the twins. It did begin – to sharpen out a bit. The blur, the grey time. It began to change. I said, 'I'm keeping them alive, I made them and I'm keeping them alive. If I can't do that I'm not even an animal.'

In the autumn I took them out in the pram sometimes. When the health visitor came she said I could try them on solids. In October they both began to have mashed banana and baby rice. They sat in high chairs, two brand-new ones Gareth had bought. I fed them one spoonful each in turn, I thought they looked like birds in a nest stretching out their heads for food. I watched them. The boy did not close his mouth, the food kept dribbling out. They tried to touch things, they pulled my hair. When they smiled at me it made me cry. I said these are children, these will grow up like Ruth and Vi, they are innocent. I wanted to sleep all the time. They smiled at each other, I saw, and I was glad of that. They seemed to like each other, perhaps that's why there had to be two. So they'd have each other's love at least.

It stopped gently. By December they were only having my milk in the night. In the day they had food, and juice. Gradually my udders subsided, gradually they took less. It was they who decided to stop. One night both of them refused the breast. I mixed them up a bottle of juice, and they drank it and went back to bed. They wouldn't take any milk after that. They had finished with me.

Ruth and Vi are pleased that I am so much better. They say, 'You see, those tablets did work in the end, you're much better than you were. Really, Mum, you really are.'

They say, 'Will you let Sarah come now? You are better, you're coping fine, you'll see. Let Sarah come then you can go out on your own a bit, now they can be left to be fed. You can stop being imprisoned in the house, it's enough to depress anyone. Let Sarah come now, please, Mum!'

They don't say they are moving back. Sarah will salve their consciences. They wanted her to come ever since the summer. Mum's sister Sarah, she can look after her, she can pick up the bits – she's sensible, she'll know what to do.

I wouldn't let them, last summer. I told them if anyone came to stay I would leave, the same day. I suppose they believed me.

Now Sarah can come. Sarah can feed the twins. I can take my tablets, three months' supply, and go.

I have been on the move again. I have driven all around, these past few days. The sun shines like steel; it comes with a razor-blade wind which slices and whips the lying snow back to life. It rises in clouds, drifts, resettles. The ploughs have been out constantly on the moortops defining roads. Here, they say, pulling behind them a clear black ribbon and a traffic jam of slow cars and lorries, this is the safe path across the snow. But when the little convoy has passed the heaped ditches of snow rise and spray up into the air, then fall again to lay false verges and edges, or to bury in a flurry the whole road. The heaps of snow at bends attract more flying snow with their bulk, and encroach into the roadway exaggerating gentle curves to hairpins. The flying snow, and sprayed-up slush from the road surface, mean that you drive blind on exposed roads.

I have driven. I have eaten. I have eaten a lot of good things in different places: home-made steak and kidney pudding, and tasty apple crumble; baked potato and steaming hot chilli, crumbly Lancashire cheese, mince tarts and custard, pie and a sea of mushy peas. Big fried breakfasts, with tomatoes, mushrooms, egg, bacon, sausage and dripping toast. Creamy yoghurt from a local dairy (the first I've had since then); crumbling fresh bread and buns and pies from small hot bakeries where men in filthy overalls crowd at lunchtimes, and pass lists of orders over the counter. On Friday I waited nearly a quarter of an hour for the man before me in the queue to have his waiting cardboard box stuffed with his mates' lunch orders, twenty-three of them. The warm bread is so good I ate a brown loaf as I drove along, tearing lumps off, and was surprised when it was all gone. Yesterday I bought all the

Sunday newspapers I could get from the local newsagent: the *Observer*, the *Mail on Sunday*, the *News of the World*, *Sunday Mirror*, *Sunday Telegraph*. I spent hours reading them. It reminded me of being a foreigner. Of going on holiday to France, and reading the papers. Not knowing the stories, not quite understanding the significance of the language, the slant.

And today it is raining. The first rain I have seen in four weeks. Deliberate, streaming rain, that pours continually from a grey sky on to the poor frozen earth, and slowly – pitifully slowly – washes away the edges of the lumps of frozen dirty snow. Gradually they are being eroded.

One more story.

The Perfect Parasite

Sally Clay believed in nature, in what is natural. She used natural products, ate wholefoods, belonged to groups whose aim is to protect the natural world from pollution and devastation by man. She expected that her body would be – natural. She was to be disappointed.

She was the only child of Maggie and Arnold Clay, both teachers. Her mother, who was more ambitious than her father, became a headmistress when Sally was twelve, and subjected Sally to considerable pressure on the subject of her future career.

But Sally's A level results were poor, and she failed to gain a place at university. Ignoring her mother's advice to get a job and retake her A levels at evening class, she left home and went to live with two other girls in a flat in a neighbouring town. One of her friends was a student at the Poly, the other worked in a bookshop.

After a few months of unemployment, and a few more as a waitress, Sally obtained a job in the bookshop alongside her friend. The shop was owned by a widow called Martha. She was well read, and an ardent feminist, with that passion of someone who has found a cause late in life. The shop became a centre for a certain kind of woman, in the town. A noticeboard was covered in cards offering lifts to Greenham, and information on demonstrations, meetings, women's groups and publications. There was a rack of alternative greetings cards; there were feminist badges and earrings; and there were books. There was political writing, sociology, women's fiction. There was poetry and keep fit, wholefood recipe books and books about witches. There were books on female sexuality, child care, and nuclear disarmament; books about subjects practical and theoretical, books for every type and kind of woman who went into the shop. There were types and kinds of women who did not go into the shop, but they were of a different class, or age, or education. Sally knew little about them. They were the women who bought their reading matter from newsagents, who read Mills and Boon. Sisters, of course – in need of liberation. But it is hard to help those who wilfully escape to the fantasy lands of *True Romance*, rather than seeking freedom.

Sally was busy. When she was not at work, she was often at a meeting. She went to her women's group, to CND, to Friends of the Earth, to yoga, and to a women's study group on sexism in children's books. When the shop next door to the bookshop fell vacant, a group of women (including Sally) formed a co-operative to raise money to open it as a women's café. They ran market stalls and raffles and held women's cabaret evenings in a local pub, and each put in two hundred pounds of her own savings. The Women's Café brought custom to the shop, the shop brought custom to the café. Business boomed.

When Sally was in her teens she had a few sexual relationships with men. As she grew into her twenties, and her political views became more defined – and her social life more completely involved with women only – she moved on to relationships with women. It was a priority with her to remain good friends with those women who were special to her, so she never lived with any of them, or allowed the relationship to become over-important. She bought a house jointly with two other women from the Women's Café Co-operative. Her life was settled and happy.

When she was twenty-eight she began to think about babies. Suddenly, they were everywhere. It was impossible to walk down the street without passing a baby staring from its pram, or one of those mysteriously self-possessed women who float past like ships in full sail, bellies marvellously rounded. Suddenly she was noticing baby clothes in shops; how miraculously tiny, those little vests and Babygros. Cycling home to visit her parents she saw lambs in the fields, butting their mothers' flanks and nuzzling for milk – feet splayed, tail stumps wriggling in frantic pleasure. The sight almost made her want to cry – and Sally was not sentimental. She examined her body in the mirror. Long and lean and well formed, with small neat breasts and generous hips – a beautiful shape, a childbearing shape, like a pear. It deserved to be used. In the shop she pored over a book of photos of babies *in utero*, curled and dreaming in their star-studded sacs, sucking their thumbs, faces blank and peaceful as icons. She wanted one. She imagined a baby cuddled in her arms, feeding from her breast; she wanted one.

Sally recognized that this was not an immature longing; she was twenty-eight. She had a satisfying job, friends, commitments. She knew she was not seeking a baby to define her own individuality. She already was, and knew what she was. No, she wanted a baby because she was a woman – it's a natural desire. And it made her glad, and proud in a way, that her personality could embrace not only feminism and her work commitments, but also the desire for self-expression through motherhood. It made her feel almost superior to those women she knew who renounced it, who found it necessary to deny part of their own natures and physicality so vehemently.

She discussed the matter with her friends – at her women's group, at home, and in the shop. Most women she knew with children had had them young, and brought them up either separate from, or despite, men. Most were married, or pregnant by accident. Very few had chosen, deliberately and singly, at a sensible age, to breed. Sally established that the women she lived with were eager to share childcare and would love a child as much as she would.

Sally decided to have a baby. She was an organized woman, and set about the task efficiently. To begin with she read everything on the subject she could find. She read about times and positions most favourable for conception (and with some scepticism, about methods for securing the conception of a female). She read about exercises, herbs and foodstuffs most helpful for the development of a healthy foetus and a relaxed supple womb; the stages of pregnancy, the stages of birth. She read women's descriptions of the births of their own children; she read about hospital mismanagement of childbirth, and the intrusion of technology. She read about the hormonal changes which affect a pregnant woman, the increased progesterone levels which flood her with calm and well-being. She read about the importance of relaxation, and she read about natural childbirth.

Then she prepared herself for the conception, as a boxer gets into training for a big fight. Her carefully balanced vegetarian diet was adhered to even more strictly than usual. Sally had been a vegetarian for years, ever since leaving home. Eating meat was unnecessary and unnatural, injurious to health. She disapproved of it on humanitarian grounds too, being opposed to factory farms and the slaughter of animals; she was also politically opposed to the guzzling of first-class protein in the Western World, when the Third World was starved for lack of the second-class protein which was used to fatten the Westerners' meat. And then there were the health hazards caused by growth hormones being pumped into cows and sheep . . . Sally could not understand how anyone could eat meat. Especially when she passed a butcher's, and saw it on the slabs: the swollen ripe livers leaking blood, the small barrel-hoop curves of lambs' ribs, with thin red flesh clinging to them. And the implements, long knife and axe to chop through bone. She averted her eyes and walked past quickly. The smell . . .

As well as yoga, she took up jogging and swimming, so that her physical fitness would be at its peak. She laid in supplies of homoeopathic substances such as *caulophyllum* to improve the muscle tone of her uterus. She made careful selection of a mate, from the three candidates within her circle of acquaintance whom she thought might oblige her, and decided on Alistair after a detailed scrutiny of his family's history and health records.

She was going to have a home delivery, assisted by her friends Mary and Sonya, and a midwife. She would not need any drugs or medical interference. Childbirth was a natural process, and Sally was going to do it naturally.

———————

For Sally it is a nice clean modern word, 'natural'. She eats food that is full of natural goodness, and wears clothes made from natural fibres. Natural now is brown bread, organic vegetables, bio-degradable washing-up liquid. On the telly it's a girl with blonde hair in a field of daisies in the sun, and she recommends a tampon or a low-calorie yoghurt. Sally thinks natural means good.

And so it does, my dear. But more than good. It meant a bigger stronger more powerful kind of good altogether, when the word was young.

NATURAL: as occurring in, sanctioned by, Nature. Right. Sweet-smelling. Morally acceptable. Knowing its place in the world. Loved by God.
UNNATURAL: against Nature. Vicious, evil, perverted. Artificial, rejected by God.

It meant order. The cosmos was a neat construction, each man and woman had a station in life, ordained and blessed by Nature. The rich man in his castle, the poor man at his gate. But once it meant order, it had to mean the opposite too. Don't you see?

Oh Sally, I learned them at school, the meanings of 'natural'. I learned from Perdita, whose noble birth shone through her shepherdess' rags. And I learned from Edmund, bastard son, spawned by a natural lust. He knew his place, he called it natural. 'Thou, Nature, art my goddess! . . . Now, gods, stand up for bastards!'

Nature in conflict with civilization – which can sanction lust only within the bounds of holy matrimony, can recognize the rights only of those born within wedlock. But Edmund was a natural son. Born of that tendency and desire within nature to proliferate, to procreate, to increase in abundance through fair means or foul – nature rampant. For civilization's sake he had to be labelled unnatural, the evil bastard who turned on his own blood, both father and brother; who forgot his place and grasped at a kingly crown. Terrible nature; the same stark Darwinian nature that menaced Tennyson with its bloody red in tooth and claw. Living nature which says eat or be eaten: rape: breed: kill: survive.

I had a rabbit when I was little. She was put with a daddy rabbit and I knew she was going to have babies. One day when I went into the shed where she lived, she was having them. Two tiny bedraggled creatures lay in the straw, and another with blood and stuff was hanging out of her. I went out quickly because I'd been told I mustn't disturb her.

When I came home from school I ran to the shed. She was sitting at the back of her cage, ears flat along her back. There were no babies. Nothing, not so much as a drop of blood on the straw. She'd eaten them – every scrap. She'd licked the straw clean.

Sally should have known about Edmund, or the
rabbit.

_____

The business with Alistair was embarrassing and felt
quite awkward. Sally's period arrived on time after the
first attempt, so in the next month they had to try several
times. Sally remained anxious, feeling sure that she would
know (as she had read some women do) the moment
conception was achieved. But her fears proved ground-
less, she was pregnant this time. And, leaving no room for
doubt, nausea and vomiting began within the fortnight.

Sally knew about morning sickness. She knew it begins
soon after conception, and generally ends at about twelve
weeks, and that it can vary in severity. She knew that for
most healthy women it is no more than a minor incon-
venience, often averted by the precaution of eating a dry
cracker in bed before getting up.

But Sally's morning sickness was not like that. She was
ill. She was sick not only in the morning, but at noon and
night – whether she had eaten anything or not, whether
she got up or not. She was sick approximately twice an
hour. She could not go to work. She felt constantly
nauseous, dizzy and faint. She lost eight pounds in the
first week. After consulting books and making her sample
a variety of herbal and homoeopathic remedies, Sonya
and Mary called in the doctor. He was sympathetic but
unhelpful. He told them that there was no need to worry
on the baby's account, since a foetus is a perfect parasite
and will take whatever it needs from the mother – only the
mother's health will suffer. There was nothing he could
safely prescribe, since there were claims that Debendox
was linked with foetal deformity. The safest course was
simply for Sally to rest as much as possible, take plenty of
fluids, and wait for the sickness to pass. If she suffered a

more serious weight loss she would have to go into hospital and be fitted to a drip, to feed her intravenously. But since this in itself would prove strange and disturbing, he preferred to leave her at home for a week or two to see if she would settle.

Sally was not used to being ill. She had never in her life felt as awful as she did now – and the sickness was unremitting, it would not even let her sleep. The days passed excruciatingly slowly, in exhausted dozing, vomiting, and tense sipping and nibbling at a wide range of drinks and foods, all of which proved equally unacceptable.

In the middle of the second month of her pregnancy Sally was taken into hospital and put on an intravenous drip. Her weight was down to six and a half stone. She lay on her back with quiet hopeless tears trickling from the corners of her eyes, hating the hospital, hating the foetus, hating herself. Having babies was not a disease – why did this have to happen to her? Her mother, who had not been informed of Sally's great decision, came to visit her and nearly cried at the sight of thin pale Sally; asked her if she had considered an abortion.

They kept her in hospital till her weight stabilized and crept up to seven stone. Back at home she continued to feel nauseous, but gradually the sickness decreased and her appetite returned. She was very tired – more tired than she had ever been before, and after attempting a couple of full days at work she could hardly drag herself about. She still hadn't regained her normal weight, so Martha suggested that she should work half days, until she felt better again.

'It's not an illness,' Sally told her. 'African women work in the fields up to and including the day their baby is born. Pregnant women are often more robust than those who are not; pregnancy is a healthy, natural state.'

'You're not African, and this isn't a field. You look

awful. Go home, have some food, and go to bed.'

Examining herself in her bedroom mirror one night Sally was shocked to notice sudden changes in her body. Her small breasts were swollen and heavy, her waist was disappearing. She knew, of course, obviously, that her body would change shape. But the speed of the meta-morphosis took her by surprise, made her feel slightly panicky, as if things had been taken out of her control.

Her plans for a home delivery were being threatened, both by the GP who had visited her, who refused to allow any first babies to be born at home ('especially to women as old as you') and by the hospital, who now had her on their books, and summoned her for four-weekly check-ups. A friend introduced her to a midwife who was in favour of home deliveries, and they agreed that the best way to manage the whole business now was probably to pretend to go along with what the hospital said. When labour started, Sally would simply stay at home. Nadine, the midwife, would be called, and the doctor could be informed afterwards that the baby had been born before Sally had time to get to hospital.

When she was four and a half months pregnant, Sally, who normally slept well, woke up in the middle of the night and could not go back to sleep. This happened four nights running. She went for long walks to tire herself out, even went swimming though she hardly had the energy for it. But she woke again next day at 2 a.m. Lying in the darkness puzzling about what was waking her, ears peeled for cats or footsteps or distant sirens, she suddenly felt an awful sensation in her belly. A sort of scramble, a shuddering shivering slither, as of something furtive and formless trying to escape. She lay still, the instant sweat boiling out of her skin, rising up in hot bubbles through her pores. It was as if her flesh were crawling – inside.

The Quickening. At four to five months, the mother-to-be first feels her baby kicking or turning. Sally recalled word for word the descriptions from her books. 'Some mothers have described that first miraculous sensation of baby stirring as being like the delicate brushing of a butterfly's wings.' As she lay paralysed and sweating on the bed, it moved again; she felt a thing that was not her shift in her belly. She shuddered involuntarily. She tried to imagine the gentle flutter of a butterfly's wings, and visualized a butterfly trapped, in there, surrounded by the folds of red meat – fluttering in a panic like a trapped bird, smashing its wings to sticky dust against the thick wet walls. She ran to the bathroom and vomited.

Back in bed she held herself stiff, waiting for the creature to move again. Tried to feel joyful, tried to feel some connection between herself and the small person who was stretching its limbs in her womb. She could feel nothing but revulsion.

There, inside her, it would grow: there, inside her, it would move. Her feelings were of no consequence to it. It had a life to live, and would live it despite her. It would wriggle and squirm repulsively in her belly whether she wanted to sleep or not. A suffocating claustrophobia descended on her and she opened the window and leant out to try and breathe. It was there. Inside her. She couldn't go out without it. Couldn't decide not to have it. Couldn't just put it down for a bit. It was there – moving, living, growing bigger all the time. She made herself breathe deeply and regularly, forcing her body to relax limb by limb. She was shaking.

It grew worse every night. As soon as she lay down to sleep it started to writhe. On a television film programme she had seen a clip from *Alien*, where a monster burst from a man's stomach. The stirrings in her own belly brought the scene vividly to mind.

When Sally was not preoccupied by the sheer physical revulsion the foetal movements caused her, she recited to herself like an incantation that she wanted this baby, she had chosen to have it, she had wanted the experience of pregnancy and motherhood, it was a part of being a woman. At night the sense of claustrophobia became more and more keen, so that she often ended up sitting by the open window, duvet wrapped round her, panting slightly and conscious of the creature growing, upwards, to increase the pressure on her lungs and constrict her breathing further. She wanted to run. The terror that gripped her could only be answered by running, fast and headlong, as far as possible.

And when she had sat panting by the window in the dark for a while, and felt her panic subsiding, she thought about how she would describe pregnancy, if someone who was writing a baby book asked her; just for balance, perhaps, she would put forward a different view.

Perhaps she would describe it as a disease. You get this disease (off men, of course – that fits). To begin with you don't know you've got it, but then it starts to make you sick. You feel dizzy and nauseous, you throw up. Perhaps your body is trying to get rid of the disease by doing this – but it won't succeed. Because you have been invaded by the perfect parasite. Your body starts to swell; breasts, belly, blow up to gross proportions – your body changes shape. Your weight increases and your back aches; your ankles swell, and varicose veins pop out on your legs. Not content with deforming your body, the disease numbs your brain, infiltrating it with chemical solutions to slow and pacify it – as they drug animals to quieten them before slaughter. You cannot shake off the lingering sluggishness. But you remember how you were before you caught this disease, and at times your rational mind panics and your swollen body balks and quivers in terror at the changes that afflict you.

All this is nothing compared to the stages that must come. When the woman is so swollen and deformed that she can scarcely stand, the creature inside her wriggles out. It takes a long time, boring out between her legs, through the most sensitive part of her body. Once delivered it clings to her like some accursed beast wished on a victim in a fairy tale. It insists on her continuous presence and attention; it feeds by chewing on her swollen nipples. And the world supports the disease in its attack upon the woman, saying how wonderful motherhood is, how you must enjoy it, how it makes you bloom. It says 'Ooh' and 'Aah' and tickles the parasite under the chin. It chuckles over sleepless nights. The woman is now destined to devote the rest of her life to nurturing the creature; her freedom, her individuality are destroyed. And the most cruel part of all is that the disease of motherhood involves the lifelong delusion of the victim. Even when the creature has taken all it can from her and moved on, she will feel the compulsive emotional need to put its interests before her own. Helplessly and pitifully she will love it, to be rewarded by its ingratitude and contempt.

Sally's intellectual pleasure in this comparison was corroded by guilt. She had chosen this, she wanted it. She had tried to get pregnant. Nothing was taking her over, she had her own life, work, friends. Care of the baby was going to be shared. It could never use her in this way. And how could a process so natural – so necessary to the survival of humanity – be seen as evil? There must be a badness within her – a failure – for her to even be able to imagine it like this. She was not doing it right. She was failing to be natural. Anyone could be a mother, women who were unhealthy, who didn't know and didn't care about their bodies, women who were undernourished and overworked, obese women, smokers – they didn't find it so hard. What was wrong with her? Pregnant women were happy. What was wrong with her?

Sally did not tell her friends about her waking nights, nor about the attacks of panic which wrung her to breathlessness two or three times a day. She was too angry and ashamed to talk about it. She made silly mistakes at work, giving customers the wrong change and forgetting titles and authors. When Martha suggested that she should stop work now, until the baby was born, Sally did not put up a fight. She seemed to be retreating into herself more and more. After trying to draw her out and being rejected, Mary and Sonya decided that Sally probably needed more personal space, at this important time in her life. She was no longer being sick, and the baby was clearly growing; what could they do? They made sure there was plenty of good food available, and they knocked on her door to chat to her on all sorts of pretexts, at evenings and weekends.

Sally hid in her room. It was her body. Her neat, well-proportioned body, her healthy flesh and skin that the creature was taking over. Soon raw red lines like welts would appear across her bulging stomach; she would be branded by stretch marks. If she had been able to tell it to stop just for a day – for a few minutes . . . But it would not. Its growth was inexorable. She was no more than its cage, trying to hold her inside walls away from its blows. Inside her own body, in the very centre of her self, her womb, something alien to herself was growing – something beyond her control. Inside her single state, a terrorist was issuing demands and making threats. Her body was in rebellion. And there were still three months to go.

Sonya and Mary were woken one night by Sally's screams. They ran to her room. She was crouching on the floor beneath the window, clutching her belly. As they ran to lift her up they saw that her thighs were streaked with watery blood, and that there was a pool of liquid on the floor. They wrapped her in a blanket and drove her straight to hospital. Then they waited in an anteroom until morning, when a nurse came to tell them that Sally had lost her baby, but that she herself would be all right.

Sally's friends were divided on how badly the miscarriage affected her. Some thought she coped very well, since she returned to work within weeks, and resumed all her previous activities. Others thought her too withdrawn – felt that she should have talked about it more. They mentioned to one another the healing effects of grieving, and the dangers of burying intense emotions. They wondered whether she would try again. Sally told them she would not.

Sally did not tell anybody why she would not try again, and perhaps she did not tell herself. She tried not to think of it, but at night pictures would come into her mind. She saw the blue-red gleaming flesh of skinned rabbits that hung on metal hooks in the butcher's shop when she was a child, the transparent membranes enclosing juices. She saw a small pale face as of someone who has never known blood, pale and bloodless and perfectly shaped as a white petal floating away on black water. She saw red meat stretching and contracting in a spastic repetition of useless movement. The heart stopped beating. The creature died.

Over the months Sally lost a lot of weight, and Mary and Sonya were very concerned. Sally angrily refused to discuss it or take advice. Now and then she ate a lot, to shut them up, then made herself sick in the toilet afterwards. At night when she undressed, she looked at her body in the bedroom mirror and saw with satisfaction that her breasts had vanished now, her rib-ridged chest was as flat as a boy's. She was glad. She didn't deserve to have breasts. She didn't deserve to be a woman.

Sometimes the girls came to visit. I'd get a phone call the night before – and then perhaps another next morning if they'd changed their minds or remembered a rehearsal or outing.

They came straight from school because it was nearer. They came in and stood in the kitchen, looking round as if they expected it to be different. I told them to sit down, and I put the kettle on. The twins were up, sitting on a rug in the corner with some toys; one kept throwing a rattle out of reach and then crying for it. Vi went to play with them. Ruth sat at the table, carefully hanging her bag and jacket over the back of the chair, like a visitor.

'How are you?' she asked.

'All right, thank you. How's school?'

'OK. We're doing a concert on Friday night.'

'We?'

'Orchestra. School orchestra. He's made me first violin because Anthea missed two rehearsals.'

'Oh. That's good.'

'We're all going to listen to her being a star,' chipped in Vi.

'Vi!' said Ruth.

'Gareth and Linda and you, you mean?' I asked.

'Yes.'

'That's nice. It'll be nice for you to have your family in the audience, Ruth.' There was a silence, broken by one of the twins starting to cry.

'I'll give them their tea,' I said. 'We can have ours afterwards. It's in the oven.' I wanted them to know I'd already made it. I mixed up some pap with hot water from the kettle and left it to cool for the twins.

'One of them's dirty, Mum, I can smell it,' said Vi. It

138

could have waited till after their tea. It was the boy. I took him to the bathroom. When I went back into the kitchen they were talking but they stopped. Vi wanted to help so she fed one while I fed the other. She kept exclaiming and laughing about how messy they were.

'Why don't you go and watch telly or something?' I said to Ruth. She was just sitting staring at the table. She went to the bottom of the stairs then turned back and went to the sitting room. I don't know why she thought of going to her old room. There was nothing in it but some old toys and books, and a few clothes she didn't like dangling in the wardrobe – mainly things I'd given her.

'How's Gareth?' I asked Vi.

'He's fine. He's going to some telly competition in Rome next week.'

'Is Linda going?'

'No, no, she's too busy at work.'

'So you and Ruth get left to your own devices quite a bit, do you?'

'We're OK. We both have lots of homework. We've been painting Ruth's room mauve. It's disgusting. She chose it.'

'Do you – who cooks?'

'Oh, Linda and Dad both cook – and sometimes we have take-aways. We're eating fine, honestly.'

'When did Gareth learn to cook?'

'He's quite a good cook, Mum. He made spaghetti bolognese the other night, you should have seen it, it was great.' The twins had finished their slop. I wiped them and took the girl out of her chair to give her a drink. The boy started to cry. It was only because Vi was there. I asked her to walk up and down with him for me.

When I'd fed them I cleared up their mess. 'I'm going to bath them, Vi. They go in the big bath now.' She might have wanted to see.

'OK Mum. I think I'll start my homework.' She sat at the table and took out her books. The twins cried as I took them to the bathroom. The boy cried all the way through his bath. The girl kept sucking the flannel. I knew she would make herself sick. I'd forgotten to get their clean sleeping suits out of the drier because the girls were there, so I had to call to Vi to get them for me. She brought the whole basket of clothes, saying she couldn't find what I wanted. She said, 'Something's run.' They were clean enough, they'd been washed.

I got them bundled up and dressed and into bed, and when I looked at my watch it was after seven. I went into the kitchen. They were both sitting at the table. Ruth said, 'Do they always cry that much?'

'I don't know. I suppose they do.' I got the casserole out for them. It would have been even longer to wait for rice to boil so I just put bread on the table.

They ate in silence.

'Have you been out anywhere nice?' I asked.

'We went to see *Close Encounters*,' Vi said.

'With Vi's special friend,' said Ruth.

'Who's Vi's special friend?'

'Well he's not a boyfriend,' said Ruth deliberately.

'Shut up!' Vi was blushing. 'He's a friend, he's just someone I happen to get on with. He is not my boyfriend. If he was my boyfriend I wouldn't go to the pictures with him with you, would I?'

Ruth shrugged.

'How's your b— Trevor, Ruth?'

'All right.'

'I – you're still seeing him, are you?'

'Yes, Mum.'

There was a silence. I cleared the plates away. I'd bought some chocolate gâteau. As I was taking it out of the fridge one of the babies began to cry.

'Haven't they gone to bed?'

'That doesn't mean they have to sleep, Ruth.' It was the girl. I paced up and down with her for a while, until she

seemed settled. Then I put her down. I was just creeping
to the door when she started up again. I sat on the bed and
gave her the breast. I was tired, I had to stop myself falling
asleep. I put her down again and crept out of the room.
They'd put the radio on, in the kitchen, I could hear the
faint hubbub of pop music in the background. They were
talking in low voices. I opened the door quietly before
they noticed I was there. They had cleared away the
dishes and Ruth had her homework out. Vi was leafing
through a magazine. I didn't know what they were talking
about, but the way the room was – the music, and the full
kitchen table, and the easy lazy conversation between
them – made me want to sit at the table and be in that
room with them. It was as if they lived there again.

We used to sit around the table a lot. I'd be reading my
bland teenage fiction, or the paper. Or the small ads.
There was a fight over the local paper every Friday night
when it arrived. I was trying to remember when it started
– I think when Vi's bike was stolen and I was looking for a
new one for her. People sell such strange things: antique
diving helmets, used corsets, gold-plated bath taps ('un-
wanted gift'). Ruth found one of the all-time gems;
'Priceless Chinese-style vase. £5.' They would snatch the
paper from each other to read them out, and we would all
giggle helplessly.

When I closed the door behind me they went quiet.

'I – would you like a drink of coffee?'

'Yes please, Mum. Is the radio too loud?'

'No. It's fine. It's nice to have it on. I seem to forget it's
there.' I made coffee and sat at the table. Ruth got on with
her homework. Vi idly showed me a couple of fashion
photos in her magazine, and asked if I liked them. Gareth
had given her some money for new clothes – she was
going shopping with Linda. One of the twins started to
cry again. I got up.

'Mum – we might get the next bus, actually,' said Ruth.

'I mean, we were quite late last night and it takes forty minutes on the bus.'

'You could stay the night,' I said. 'If you wanted. I mean, there's plenty of sheets and blankets.'

'It's OK thanks, Mum. I've got to take my violin to school tomorrow anyway and it's at ho— at Dad's.'

'Of course.'

'You must be tired, with these two – you probably want to go to bed early too. Don't worry, we'll let ourselves out. See you.'

'Yes, see you Mum.' Vi not looking up from her magazine. They would be embarrassed if I kissed them.

The one that was crying had a full nappy, again. I changed it and got it back to bed. I could hear the radio still playing softly. But when I hurried back to the kitchen, the radio was playing and the light was shining in an empty room.

Wed. March 5

It's still raining. The snow diminishes slowly. I've been here since Monday, it's a quiet, comfortable place, although my room is cold. The dining room has ten tables but there are only four of us staying at present: a couple who are house-hunting and spend hours at the table poring over local papers, maps and estate agents' notes – and a solitary, wretched-looking man, perhaps a salesman of some sort. There is a fire in the dining room, and I have taken to sitting by it after my meals, watching the coals collapse and the flames leap. My money will run out soon. There is £84 left of the £500 I took out before I left. I could take out some more, but I don't think I will. She is only charging £11 for bed and breakfast and evening meal – and the petrol tank is nearly full.

I sat by the fire after breakfast this morning to drink my

second cup of tea. The couple crackled their papers and muttered together, and planned their route of inspection for the day (they don't look wealthy. I wonder if they are agents for someone else?) The wretched man messed with his breakfast then left it. I sat staring at the fire and sipping hot tea and when I next looked up the couple had gone too. It was nine o'clock but barely light outside, and the rain streamed down the window so continuously that it was as if we were submerged in some great river. I heard a slight noise and realized that the landlady was clearing the breakfast tables, very quietly and efficiently. She smiled at me then carried on with her work as if I wasn't there. After a while (she'd washed up, I suppose) she returned with a bucket and cloth. She didn't even glance in my direction this time – just made straight for the wide plate-glass windows at the far end of the room. Through the streaming glass there is a view of a small grey garden, the muddy rawness of a building site, and dim wet hills in the distance. She wrung her cloth in the bucket, and began to clean the windows. I think she had forgotten that I was there; she moved loosely, easily, with no self-consciousness. She is a big woman, tall and well built, with faded blonde hair. In her late forties, I should guess. She looks used to plenty of exercise. I watched her stand on tiptoes and reach to the tops of the windows, making huge rounds with her arms. Then she turned, stooped, dipped and wrung the cloth. She was wearing baggy trousers which were gathered at the waist, and a man's shirt. She wasn't fat but she had a rounded tummy – a clearly defined, rounded little pot belly, swelling under the gathered waist of her trousers – and heavy, slightly drooping breasts, outlined against the window as she raised her arm to sweep across. She reminded me of primitive figures of women, with round ripe bellies and breasts; childbearing women, symbols of fertility. There was something innocent and unashamed about her body, she did not try to disguise it, she did not care that it was not like a model's. And the shape it had, came from the use it had been put to; it had worn to a comfortable shape.

A childbearing body. The children grew in it, I fed them. Even the twins grew in peace, were delivered safely into the world. Even though I was at my wits' end, my body fed them. Went on making milk mechanically, knew what to do, despite me. Oh Sally, I'm sorry.

I've spent the morning reading all this. From the beginning – Sun. Feb. 2, when I first set off in the car, in the
snow – till yesterday. A month of fun with Marion. I think
it's more than enough.

You haven't finished the list.

No – but there's no end to the list, that's obvious now. It
would go on for pages – for years, for as long as my life.
Unless it is complete the list is a distortion, and the only
way to complete it would be to write continuously.

The others are finished: David and Amanda, Alice
Clough and Ellen, Leonie and Gary, Sally Clay. Their
stories are complete. Thanks to me: I've sewn them up
tight. Drawn significances, illustrated their beginnings,
signalled their endings. I made their shape, I made them.
Paper children, I made them.

Much more than my self-willed flesh-and-blood children. Poor paper children under my control. Fragile,
tissue-thin, tear-absorbing children whose lives are con-
fined within the white coffin-rectangles of the pages
where I have set them down. I made them unhappy.

But in transferring pain to them, I exorcise it for myself.
Isn't that how it's supposed to work? David loses the
daughter he loves too much. Ellen Clough's possessive-
ness destroys her daughter's life. Leonie knows the only
way to protect a child completely from an evil world is to
kill him. Sally thought she was in control, and that
motherhood is an instinctive state of grace.

Oh Marion! How neat! How sweet and trim as apple-
pie neat. Nothing like someone else's troubles indeed!
What a ham. And the corners she cut! The sleights of hand
she used. The bloody cheap tricks, the creaking scenery.
Was Alice dead, at the end of her story? Where was she?

What happened next? It doesn't matter, says Marion loftily. Whether she was dead or alive is irrelevant, the story has made its point.

Oh yes? And when your story has made its point, my dear – whatever that may be – do you think it will matter to you if you're dead or alive? Or will that be irrelevant?

And Sally; did she die? Anorexia is not easily curable, but if circumstances changed . . . Perhaps six months later she moved to a new job, and started an Open University course, and was so exhilarated by the change of scene and intellectual stimulation that she forgot to starve herself, and became plump, well-balanced and powerful. Or maybe a man (could even be he's-only-a-sex-object-Alistair) was kind to her, and after a decent interval of time, discussed with her the idea of living together and sharing responsibility for a child in the time-honoured way; and she had a cheerful second pregnancy, and a lovely baby, and everything was fine. Until she fell in love with Alistair's sister and he wanted custody of the child, and . . . and . . . so on.

Leonie. I can see her now, not dead, nor imprisoned, nor insane. She's sitting with one of her grandchildren on a bench in the park, reading him a comic and feeding him Jaffa Cakes from her big tartan shopping trolley. They laugh together when a greedy duck flaps out of the pond and waddles across the path to beg a biscuit. She doesn't put flowers on Gary's grave. What's the point?

All right then. Cheap tricks. False endings. Crude shapes. Where's the good in it? What have you been doing, Marion, all the time you've sat with a pen in your hand and words uncurling methodically across the page behind it?

Making patterns. Exercising control. Rewriting the world so that its knocks are well timed and tragic. Instead of being so destroyingly continuous that they merely numb.

Lists are not tragic. Ruth and Vi and Paul and Penny and I, we are never at the end of the story, I am not allowed to grieve.

And when it is done, all over and done, and a story-teller, picking over the bones of my life, sees a clear pattern, a rounded story – then you will know (who will know? you'll be dead) what a lie the story is, and how neat, and satisfying, and necessary are the lies of fiction, which impose order on the world, and punctuate it, and save us from these bloody awful lists.

Tell me a story. I told them stories all the time. From known starting points: Winnie the Pooh, Peter Pan, Red Riding Hood, Alice. All my stories were sequels. They liked characters they knew, and so did I. Hop o' my Thumb was a great favourite, all through one winter, only deposed by the Borrowers, who were just as small but pandered to their growing desire for realism (in detail, at least). I liked Hop o' my Thumb, I liked him a lot. I still know his original story by heart.

Hop o' my Thumb

Once a poor woodcutter and his wife had seven sons. They were all fine strong boys except for the youngest, and he was tiny – no bigger than his father's thumb. So they called him Hop o' my Thumb. His brothers used to mock him for his puny strength. 'What use will that fellow ever be?' they cried, and laughed till the little house shook.

The woodcutter and his wife were very poor, and one winter they could not feed their sons; there was not a scrap of food in the house. The couple sat up all night worrying about what to do, and at last decided to lead their sons deep into the forest and there leave them to their fate. 'Anything would be better,' said their mother, 'than watching them starve to death before our very eyes.' Hop o' my Thumb heard that his parents were in serious discussion, and so he hid himself beneath his father's chair and listened to their plan. Early next morning he filled his pocket with white pebbles from the path, and when the family set off into the forest, Hop o' my Thumb dropped a pebble behind him every few paces. When at last the boys realized that they were lost, and their parents gone, they began to wail and cry. But Hop o' my Thumb said, 'Don't worry, brothers, if we follow this trail of white pebbles we shall soon be safely home.' And this is what they did.

The parents, in the meantime, had been repaid some money that was owed to them, and had been able to buy enough food to stock every shelf in the larder. Bitterly did they regret abandoning their children; each began to blame the other for so foolish a plan. How happy they were, when their sons, led by little Hop o' my Thumb, arrived home safe and sound that night.

———————

Clever little Hop o' my Thumb, smallest of children, knew so much better than his parents did. No wonder the girls liked him. Hop o' my Thumb at school. Hop o' my Thumb gets trapped in the fridge. Hop o' my Thumb and the pirate ship. Tell me a story.

Paper children. I used to play with paper dolls. There was a craze for them when I was a child; fold the paper, draw an outline doll with hands touching the edges of the paper, and cut around the shape. You need sharp scissors, to cut through all the folds. Unfold, and there's a string of dancing figures holding hands. I became good at it, cut intricate hairstyles and frilly dresses, even cut little diamond patterns in their skirts. When I made a chain of them for Ruth as a toddler, she was delighted. I spread them on the table in front of her and she pored over them. Then she grabbed a crayon from her box and began drawing eyes and grinning mouths.

'What are you doing?' I cried.

She just beamed at me – it was a silly question. But my dolls had always had blank faces, I never drew on them. I couldn't help feeling Ruth was spoiling them. It wasn't what you do with paper dolls.

March 7

Ruth and Mum.

She had the first stroke when Ruth was thirteen. After a few weeks they sent her home. She'd lost the use of her legs but there was nothing they could do. Dad wanted to look after her, and the district nurse came in to give her baths. I took days, adding up to weeks, off work.

She didn't know how to be an invalid. She hated it. I used to send Dad out – shopping, for a walk, over to see the neighbours – anything to get him out of the house for a break – and as soon as he was gone she would start.

'I don't know why you let me go on like this, Marion. If I was an animal, you'd have me put down. You wouldn't let a dog live the life that I do.'

'Mum,' I said brightly, 'don't be so daft. Don't talk so silly. You're still alive and we're all glad. What will Dad do if you die? You talk as if there's nothing you can do – you've still got your mind, that's the most precious thing – you can enjoy other people, read, watch telly – you can knit and –'

She stared at me with such contempt I did not know what to say. She was not afraid of death. Her bladder control was impaired and she used to cry when she wet herself. She couldn't bear the indignity.

I tried being bright and cheery. I tried ignoring her.

149

Then I shouted at her and told her to stop being such a self-pitying cow when we were all trying to help her and make her happy. I told her she was selfish and that she was ruining Dad's life.

Nothing worked. We knew each other too well.

'How would you feel?' she said. I begged her not to kill herself, and she laughed at me.

I don't know why Ruth first came with me. For a while I refused to take the girls because I didn't want them to see her like that, to hear her saying those things. But one day, for whatever reason, thirteen-year-old Ruth came with me. I packed Dad off to chop some kindling, and got a brief progress report from him, outside the back door. When I went back into the house Ruth was sitting by Mum's bed reading to her from an exercise book. I went into the kitchen to make a stew for Mum and Dad's tea, and left the door open. It was a history essay about the First World War. When Ruth finished Mum said:

'Don't they teach you anything these days? What happened to English grammar? I suppose you've never heard of a split infinitive, have you?' She went back over the essay correcting points of style and grammar – I heard Ruth interrupting her and standing up for her own version a few times. Then they started talking about the war. Mum was telling her about her father, Grandpa Poyser who I never met, who survived being gassed in the trenches when Mum was three years old. I finished making the stew, made a pot of tea, and took them a cup each. They were still chattering busily. So I took my tea outside with Dad's, and sat with him on the step.

On the way home Ruth was very perky. She told me she had to do an oral history project, a tape of an old person talking about the past. She was going to use Grandma. She would ask her about the Second World War, or her education – or fashion, what did I think?

Next time I went she came with me and offered Mum a

choice of subjects. They finally decided together on *A woman's place in World War Two*, and Ruth interviewed her for hours. She found out about land girls, munitions factory workers, evacuated chidren, shopping and cooking on rations, clothing coupons and wartime fashions – a vast ragbag of information which took them days to unearth. A book was added to the tape; Mum made Dad go through trunks and cases to find old photos, recipes and newspaper cuttings. For two months, Mum did not talk of dying. One night on the way home I said to Ruth,

'What are we going to do when this project of yours is finished, Ruthie? How are we going to keep Grandma out of mischief?'

She laughed. 'Don't worry, Mum. I'll invent something else.'

When Mum died that summer it was clean and quick, the second stroke killed her outright. She was happily occupied writing her childhood memoirs, at the time, with pen and ink illustrations by Ruth.

Sat. March 8

The snow has retreated. Mainly thanks to rain, which sullenly washed it away over days; since Thursday, the rainfall has been interrupted by spokes of steely sunlight, which shine icily from a white sky into puddles, wet roads, sodden hills, and make eyefuls of splintered glass. The remains of the snow are dirty white patches which glint on moortops, and grey decaying mounds (which I have twice mistaken for dead sheep) by the roadsides. It's done for, at last.

I went for a walk today, around the nearby reservoir. It is one of three flooding the valley between the moors; edged by a neat Waterways road and, to one side, a sloping hillside divided into empty faded fields. On the other side the ground rises steeply to the moor, with overhanging rocks and loose stone, sharp dark shadows. Leached of colour, the land appears dead, sparsely covered by sodden washed-out tufts of last year's coarse grass. I walked towards the water. Most of the surface is still covered with sheet ice, but it is broken near the shore – it's come adrift from the land. The sheets are cracked in places, and jostle each other uneasily on the moving water.

Near down by the shore, there is a continuous sound of ice tinkling. I tried to think what it sounded like: windchimes, tiny bells, the noise icicles would make if tapped together. But what it sounds most like, of course, is what it is: lumps of ice chinking together and melting in liquid. A thousand well-iced glasses of gin and tonic simultaneously raised and gently swirled – the clear tinkle of cube against cube and cube against glass. All across the reservoir, and amplified in the clear still air of the valley, the edges of the ice floes are cracking and exploding as they melt, in a wide chorus of gentle chinks and tinkles. The ice is singing.

At the farther, more sheltered end of the reservoir the sun is bright, the ice-tinkle distant. Small waves lap brightly on the shore. There is a steep man-made slope down to the road below, and a flock of sheep stand motionless in the sunshine, each one fixed to the spot by a small dark shadow falling to the left; as if some careful child had glued them in place, and left a pressure thumb print.

I shall go home. That is, back to the twins. For the following reasons (and let me be clear about this, clear-eyed and certain that there is no self-deception involved):

Because there is no alternative.

Because I am tired of driving about, and staying in other people's rooms, and having my meals cooked for me.

Because the twins are my children. Ruth and Vi were instantly precious, and then so burnished and gilded by my love that their value became terrible. I wouldn't change that – even if it was wrong, even though it was wrong. I'll pay for it. I must, as best I can, make precious the twins. Dare to make them something terrible to lose. There is no alternative. The alternative is emptiness – nothing.

Because I don't want to die.

And (be clear. Be honest, Marion, be steady) these are not reasons for returning:

I am not returning with joy or hope in my heart, thinking it will all be different. I am not thinking the twins will let me sleep, or think, or live. I am not returning thinking Ruth and Vi will come home. I am not thinking of Gareth. I am not returning under any illusion that anyone will be pleased about what I've done. I am returning apologetic for the upsets I have caused by my sudden, irresponsible absence.

I am not returning home because it will be spring and my heart and sorrows have melted with the snows. The poor battered land shows no signs of spring, encourages no such thought. The forecasts speak of more snow before March is out. Spring will come, but two seasons later, so will another winter, just as cold. The earth won't stop turning for me.

I am returning because I am not a story. There is no controlled shape – beyond the circle my journey away and back will describe. That is a freedom. My life goes on, shapelessly, raggedly, from day to day. I don't know what will happen. But my life goes on.